Lotogettar

by

Valerie Soovajian

DORRANCE PUBLISHING CO
EST. 1920
PITTSBURGH, PENNSYLVANIA 15238

Dorrance Publishing Co
585 Alpha Drive
Pittsburgh, PA 15238
Visit our website at www.dorrancebookstore.com

ISBN: 979-8-8868-3277-8
eISBN: 979-8-8868-3672-1

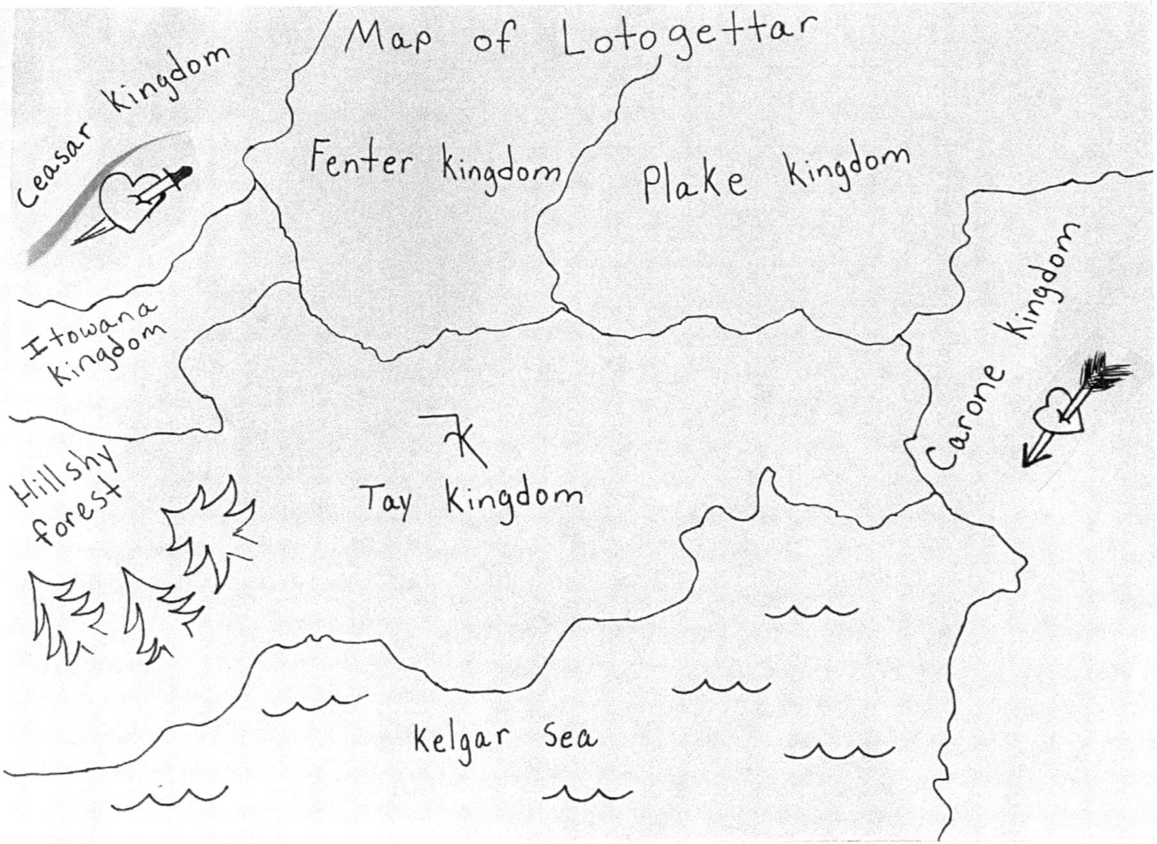

Map of Lotogettar
Ceasar Kingdom
Fenter kingdom
Plake Kingdom
Carone Kingdom
Itowana Kingdom
Tay Kingdom
Hillshy forest
Kelgar Sea

Chapter One

"Everyone loves a good adventure and telling their stories about them. They could be real or fake…happy or sad. Or they can be filled with excitement. Mary's story was the exact same way except filled with love. It all started back in 1957…."

"Good morning, everyone in America! This is your host John Daney broadcasting live from—"

The sound of static cutting off the radio filled the silent room, making the redhead who sat nearby lose all thoughts that filled her head. Mary sighed as she heard loud clanking heels approach.

"Damn it! We just got this thing last month and it's been acting up all week." Annoyance laced in Rose's voice. Mary watched as her mom hit the sides of the radio.

"You're gonna break it even more if you keep hitting it like that," Mary said

"What other options are there? It's not just ours, you know…Jennifer across the street is having problems…so is Mrs. Lawrence," her mom replied.

"It's probably just the rain."

"We get rain all the time and it has never affected anything. If your father were still here, he would know what to do."

A faint smile fell on Rose's lips as she thought about her late husband, Jack. Jack had died fighting in the recent war just when Mary was seven years old. Rose remembers that day like it was yesterday. Just one knock at the door changed her life. Mary ran as fast as her tiny feet could take her to the door like she had done for six months asking if Daddy was finally home. Rose only peered down at her daughter's little figure with tears in her eyes having to explain that she wouldn't see her father for a very long time. Together they sat on the wooden floor crying in each other's arms. It had been eleven years since then.

"You take after him, you know. You got his red hair, green eyes, smile, and love for adventure."

Mary smiled at her mother's words.

"Could I…?" She gestured to the front door.

"Go. It's a nice day…just don't get your dress dirty."

Mary sat up with a smile and ran towards the front door, where she put on her white sneakers. Rose didn't quite approve of the shoes, always saying, "Sneakers are for men." But Mary insisted they were perfect for adventuring through the woods.

And off she went, out the front door and onto her front porch. Mary stood there for a second and just stared out at the world. Kids were playing kickball and riding bikes in the street. The sun was shining down onto the wet glistening grass from the previous day's weather. Running down the porch steps and stone pathway, Mary turned the corner continuing down Borrows street. The town she lives in is a small one called Unbures town in upstate New York. A small populated area where everyone knows everyone.

Arriving moments later at Meadowbrook Park, Mary walked along past the new playground that was opened only two weeks ago and wandered onto a dirt pathway that led to the woods. The sun shimmered through the green leaves of the large oak trees surrounding her. Wandering farther through the woods she ran up a hill to a grassy meadow. She lay down onto the soft, damp grass, ignoring her mother's words and not caring if her dress got dirty.

Mary viewed the sky above leaning her head back into her hands.

White fluffy clouds of different shapes and sizes moved slowly in the blue sky. It was just like old times when Mary's father took her out to this spot. Her father would point out clouds that appeared as the shape of a castle or a dragon. He would then tell her stories of big castles, monstrous dragons, strong warriors, brave princes, kings, and queens, including Mary herself as a princess.

Mary closed her eyes as a cool breeze blew past. Taking a deep breath the scent of rain and grass filled her lungs. Being out here gave Mary a peaceful state of mind where all her worries went away. Soon the clouds grew darker, covering the sky, and the wind picked up speed. Mary's long red hair blew in different directions along with the wind. A single cold, small raindrop fell on her nose.

CRACK! BOOM!

The sound of thunder frightened her a little but she soon relaxed. She stayed lying there stretching out her arms as more small raindrops slowly fell onto her porcelain skin.

The rain began to pour down harder. Mary stood up laughing as her dress got soaked by the water and her hair turned a darker shade. She ran down the small clearing and down the dirt path that was turning muddy, staining her white shoes. Arriving home Mary walked up to the porch about to open the door just as her mother opened it for her.

"Oh my goodness look at you. You're a mess! And take those muddy shoes off! Don't let them dirty my floor," Rose shrieked.

Sending her an apologetic smile, Mary mumbled a quick, "Sorry," hiding her smirk as she walked in and placed her shoes on the small shoe mat.

"Just…wait here."

Rose sighed, pinching the bridge of her nose as she rushed off to get towels. Quickly she came back placing a towel on top of the muddy shoes and one around Mary. Walking past her mother she went to sit on the couch before Rose shrieked once more pulling her straight back up.

"You're gonna get my couch dirty!"

She wiped the grass and dirt off the blue skirt of Mary's dress

"I want you straight in the bath. I'll put on a pot of tea so you don't get sick."

Mary rolled her eyes and left the room without a word, heading to the bathroom and running a warm bath.

Wake up.

Eat breakfast.

Adventure through the woods.

Get yelled at for getting her dress dirty.

And going to bed.

Mary was starting to get bored with the same events repeating every day. She wanted something different.

Laying in her bed, she started to doze off after hours of trying to get sleep without thinking over every little detail in her life. The same dream that always occurred every night played in her mind. It had started when she first lost her dad.

The dream was of her and a boy that she had never seen before. She was always laying in the nameless boy's lap and could never see her surroundings but only ever felt cold. The boy would look down at her with tears in his eyes saying he was sorry and that he had failed her. Then she would wake up forgetting his face except for his bright blue eyes.

***

Getting up and ready the next morning, Mary walked into the kitchen to see her mother cooking pancakes.

"Good morning, sweetie. Could you get me a cup of orange juice?"

Too tired to speak, she opened the refrigerator and went to grab the orange juice only to feel nothing in her grasp.

"There's no more."

Rose sighed.

"Could you go to the store? I have a list of groceries we need—hold on…let me get it. Here, flip those please."

Rose handed Mary the spatula before leaving to her office in search of the grocery list.

She began to flip the pancakes as she waited for her mother to come back. Mary began to reverie about her dream. Trying hard to remember what the boy looked like, she closed her eyes. A flash of silky blond hair suddenly appeared for a quick second before disappearing and immediately broke from her thought as a whiff of burning food caught her nose.

"Shoot."

Mary looked down at the now-burnt pancakes.

"What's burning!" Rose yelled, running back into the kitchen, panicked.

"Sorry."

Rose sighed, catching sight of the charred pancakes.

"That was the last of the pancakes…but it's fine. I'll make more once I get the ingredients since we're all out," Rose said, handing over a small list.

Mary set down the spatula, took the list, and ran to the front door.

"And tuck that shirt in!" Rose shouted.

"Yeah…yeah."

She stumbled out of the house as she tucked her shirt into her pink skirt. Walking over to the side of the house and hopping onto her bike, she adjusted her skirt so that it would not get caught on the wheel. She then put the list securely in her pocket and sped off down the road to the store.

It was another sunny day, which would most likely turn into a stormy day like yesterday. So Mary enjoyed it while she could.

Pulling up to the local Shoprite ten minutes later, Mary leaned her bike on the side of the wall near other bikes and strolled into the big shop. She took the list out of her pocket peering down at it, reading her mother's cursive lettering, and wandering down the aisle.

"Milk, flower, eggs—"

"Need help with anything, ma'am?" a deep voice suddenly interrupted her.

She smiled brightly and looked up to see her friend Max.

"Hey, Maxy! I haven't seen you since last month."

Mary jumped into her friend's arms, hugging him tightly. He hugged her back placing his head on top of her head. Pulling away, Mary took in his appearance. His brown hair had grown a bit of a wave and he had dark bags under his bright green eyes.

"You look tired…are you okay?"

"I'm fine. I just haven't gotten much sleep since I've got this job…don't worry."

"Well, of course, I'm gonna worry. Anyways…how have you been?"

"I've been fine, but I'm sorry I haven't been able to hangout much," he said with a tired smile.

"Don't worry…it's fine. Never affected us before," Mary replied, picking up a bag of flour from the shelf and placing it in the red basket she had grabbed on her way in. She opened her mouth to continue to talk when the manager walked past.

"Get back to work, Mr. Fends!"

Max sighed. "Well, guess I gotta get back to this." He motioned to the canned food he had to restock and continued. "But we should hang out tomorrow. I can take a sick day."

"Well, then…I'll see you tomorrow, Maxy."

He rolled his eyes in annoyance at the nickname she had called him since second grade and hugged her one last time.

From there she went on her way in search of the rest of the groceries and left, placing the heavy bags into the basket of her bike. Mary decided to walk her bike back since it would be too heavy to control with the groceries.

Nearing her home, Mary saw an unfamiliar car parked out front. She frowned in confusion as she walked up to the shiny pink Cadillac convertible. Mary took the groceries, dropping her bike on the front lawn of her house.

"Hey, Mom, I'm home! By the way who's car is that outside?" she asked as she entered the house, walking straight to the kitchen to put the groceries away.

"That's your graduation present," a new voice called back. Mary gasped with a big smile, knowing exactly who that was.

"Aunt Debbie!"

She ran into the living room, seeing her mom and aunt both wearing the same smiles as they held their cups of coffee. Mary almost could not tell them apart since the two were identical twins. Same blonde hair and blue eyes. Even their noses were the same.

Debbie quickly placed her mug down and stood up from her seat, pulling Mary into a hug.

"I haven't seen you since you were starting the eighth grade. I've missed you so much."

"I missed you too!"

Pulling away, Debbie wore a bright smile. "So, do you like your present?"

"That car…it's for me?" Mary asked unsure.

"Yes! Of course it's for you."

"I love it! But that's too much…you didn't have to."

Debbie waved her off. "Oh don't be silly. You've graduated. You deserve it."

"Thank you."

Debbie was the outgoing, fun aunt. Her personality was the complete opposite from Rose, who was a content person that could be easily annoyed by the littlest thing.

"Oh and there's another gift!"

Mary smiled and shook her head.

"Aunt Debbie…I think the car is more than enough."

"Honey…you will love this gift even more."

Rose exchanged an excited glance with her sister.

"Well, then, what is it?" Mary smiled back confused.

"You will get to go back home with me. The best part is you'll get the chance to go to college," Debbie hesitantly announced.

The smile on Mary's face fell. "That's in Florida…I'll probably be there for four years."

"Well, you could go for two years, but I would rather you go for four years. Isn't that great? You'll get the chance to do something I never got to do!" Rose said, unaware of her daughter's dislike of this conversation.

"I guess…but four years is a long time and I was never interested in going to college in the first place." Mary was starting to grow stressed.

"Come on, Mary, this is a once-in-a-lifetime thing. That writing career you want so badly will just be a waste of time and get you nowhere," Rose replied, getting agitated.

"Yeah, the teachers made that very clear before I graduated," Mary said with a crack in her voice, growing more upset. It hurt when people said that. Always doubting her. Debbie interrupted, sensing Mary's distraught reaction.

"Rose…I told you this was a bad idea."

Tears welled up in Mary's eyes as she scoffed, "Of course it was *your* idea."

"Watch the attitude! You leave tomorrow, so I suggest you start packing." Rose was getting more disappointed with her child.

Mary's breathing grew shaky as she practically yelled, "Tomorrow!? I can't just leave like that. Mom…are you listening? I can't just leave without a word and who knows how long it will be till I come back home!"

"Don't you dare raise your voice at me! I am very disappointed in you. You are going whether you like it or not!" Rose yelled over her.

Mary frantically wiped the tears off her face. "I hate you."

Rose's heart broke a bit. She didn't mean to upset Mary. "Where are you going?" she yelled, nervously watching her daughter walk to the front door.

"I just need a moment!" Mary yelled back, slamming the door behind her.

Her thoughts ran wild as she thought over everything in their discussion. Mary didn't want to go to college. She wanted to write books and be a famous author, but people would always say that it was unrealistic or that it would be hard for her. They always doubted her, bringing up all of the negativity and making her lose all motivation she held. The tears would not stop falling and Mary ran to the park.

As soon as she stepped into the woods, it started to rain heavily as usual. Between her tears and the rain falling violently, Mary's vision clouded over, as she grew deeper each minute into the woods, but soon stopped as she realized something. Wiping away the water in her face she squinted her eyes to see she was surrounded by trees. Nothing else could be seen besides the thick wooded area. Mary did not recognize anything. She was lost. Panic overtook her as she ran in a random direction hoping it was the right way.

Slosh! Slosh!

Mary frantically ran through wet mud each step she took. Mud and water splashed all over her and just as she made another turn, Mary tripped over a rock, hitting her head on a tree stump. A loud yelp escaped her mouth before she blacked out.

Chapter Two

The sound of sniffing was what woke Mary. Sitting up, she examined her surroundings. Tall thick trees covered the small grassy area where she sat blocking away the sun that peeked through just a bit. A few feet away, she spotted a small pond. The water glistened like diamonds as small red and orange fish swam calmly around. Another sniffing noise and something nudging her head caused her to turn around to come face-to-face with a horse. Mary jumped back a little but soon relaxed, reaching out to pet the horse's brown silky face. Letting out a low neigh, the horse lowered its head to devour a purple flower that stood tall above the dewy grass. A calming sensation came over Mary; wherever she was made her feel like she was at home. It was reticent until…

"Nayle! Nayle mante lay!" a deep rich voice yelled out.

Mary looked all around for wherever this stranger was. Footsteps were heard running closer to where she was. Looking to a nearby bush, Mary pondered if she should hide. She hurriedly stood up about to jump behind the bush before a boy jumped out in front of her. Startled, they both let out a short scream, falling backwards onto their backs and groaning in pain.

Mary had a growing headache as she leaned on her elbows rubbing a small lump on her head. Looking to see where the boy had fallen, she saw he had already stood up. The boy, yet to be named, walked over to Mary. She backed up a little, not trusting him. Seeing this, he sent her a comforting smile, reaching his hand out to help her up.

"Lye bea…gela sho kit?" the boy said in a strange language. It almost sounded like he had a British accent.

"Uh…is that Spanish?" she asked, unsure and grasping his hand. The boy sent her an odd look and pulled her up.

"Spinkish? I've never heard such a silly word," he replied.

Laughing at his mistake Mary was now face to chest with this mysterious boy. Taking a step back she took in his appearance. He looked to be about her age and was taller than her, thin, and strongly built. Mary would be lying if she wasn't intimidated. Though there was something about him.

Something familiar.

He had lengthy bright blond hair that landed above his shoulders and piercing blue eyes. His white skin seemed to glow in the sun that peeked through the trees above. He wore a silk blue tunic and brown pants with leather boots, and a shiny dagger was hooked loosely onto his pants. Mary stood in confusion. People did not wear outfits like this. Who was he? And where was she?

The boy spoke, breaking Mary away from her thoughts.

"But seriously…my lady…are you alright? That looked like a rough landing…and your dress is completely covered in mud." She went to reply before he continued on. "Was someone after you? I will take care of them." He placed his hand on the hilt of the dagger peering around his surroundings on alert.

"My lady…?" Mary mumbled confused. *Who says my lady…?* "I'm fine…I just don't know exactly where I am." She looked around then back to the boy.

Breaking from his alarmed stance, he became confused as well.

"Why you're in the Hillshy Forest."

"Hillshy? I've never heard of that place." She became confused. Only a minute ago, she was in the woods of New York.

"Everyone's heard of Hillshy! It is one of the most famous forests in *Lotogettar*. It's peaceful during the day showing it's true calm beauty, but at night strange activity goes on…. Where are you from? Your accent tells me you are not from around here and what's your name?" he asked, looking at her strangely.

"I'm Mary…Mary Clemmons. I'm from New York. But I've never heard of a place called Lotogettar either." She sent him a confused laugh.

"Mary…what a beautiful name. But there is no such place as New York here," he said, denying the existence of this so-called *New York* place and continued. "It is lovely to meet you, Lady Mary! I am Noah Tay," he stated proudly.

Mary held out her hand with a smile. "It's nice to meet you too."

Noah looked down at her hand and pulled it up to his lips, gently kissing her knuckles. Mary blushed. This was quite odd and new for her. Nobody had ever kissed her hand let alone anyone else's.

"Come along, then. Let's take you back to my home so you can get cleaned." Noah placed a hand on her shoulder, guiding her out of the woods. "Nayle! Come!" He whistled for the horse to follow as they continued to walk down a wide stone pathway.

Mary looked around at the tall dark green trees in awe. The trunks and branches were wide and huge. She had never seen trees that big before.

She observed as a family of squirrels ran up one tree, disappearing into a dark hole. They came to a stop at an exit of thick brown branches that twisted together, creating a tall arch. They stepped out of the forest into a bright grassy hill. Noah grabbed Mary's hand and tugged her up the hill with a childish smile.

"Come on it's just right over the hill. Oh and be careful not to step on any snakes," he said, quickly running up the hill, tugging her along.

"Snake's! What—"

She stopped short as they reached the top. Mary stared in wonder at the beautiful sight that appeared before her. A castle, tall and strong made of what looked to be glass sat there peacefully in the field. It was guarded by a white thick glass wall that gleamed as the sun fell down on it. Next door was a lavish town of wooden houses guarded by a cobblestone wall. Everything was yore.

"Wow."

"Wow, indeed," Noah whispered back, staring lovingly at her.

Mary blushed a bit, catching his stare and took a step forward towards the castle speaking softly, "This can't be real? I must be dreaming."

"It's as real as your beauty," Noah replied with a shy smirk.

Laughing slightly Mary blushed even more, "You must flirt with all the girls here."

"Well, being the prince, all the girls are always trying to flirt with me."

Mary turned to the smirking boy. "You're a prince…? What's that like?" She looked back at the castle, studying it like it was a beautiful painting.

Noah frowned, wondering why she wasn't throwing herself at him or judging him. "You're different than the others," he blatantly said, walking past her. "Come along, then."

They walked along a smooth stone pathway as the horse trotted past them to the large front gates. Arriving face-to-face with the glass gates, a loud voice spoke firmly from above.

"*Valta! Layar shyar!*" (Stop! Who goes there!)

Guards were stationed in the towers above on the glass walls peering down at the two and pointing their bows at them ready to shoot.

"*Pa lay shor patays! Jiy shor Kinsi,*" (Put your weapons down! It is your prince) Noah shouted up to them.

The head guard motioned for them to put their weapons down and replied back, "*Shor quental cado mora lay.*" (Your Highness…please forgive me.) The guard's eyes moved to Mary, eyeing her suspiciously. "*Layar ji bei?*" (Who is she?)

Noah turned to Mary with a soft smile. "This is my friend…Mary. She is no threat to me or the kingdom."

The guard nodded in approval. "*Topian Jate!*"

The sound of wheels turning filled their ears as the gates slowly opened. A gust of wind blew past them as they fully opened. Even closer to the castle now, Mary saw how much bigger it really was. It was unnaturally taller and wider than normal buildings she has seen in the city. As she walked through the gates with Noah, another guard came over, bowed, and collected the horse, taking it to a stable that hid behind the wall.

"What does topen jate mean?"

Noah chuckled a bit. "*Topian jate,*" he corrected. "It means 'open the gate.' Looks like you have a lot to learn if you're going to be staying in Tay kingdom for a while. That's our language. Tayens language. It originated from our ancestors." He then motioned to the castle as he continued. "This castle has been here for centuries. It's the largest castle on Lotogettar and has been the same since. The only thing we recently changed was the color of our flag."

He pointed to a large green flag hung high above the front doors to the castle that blew flapped in the wind.

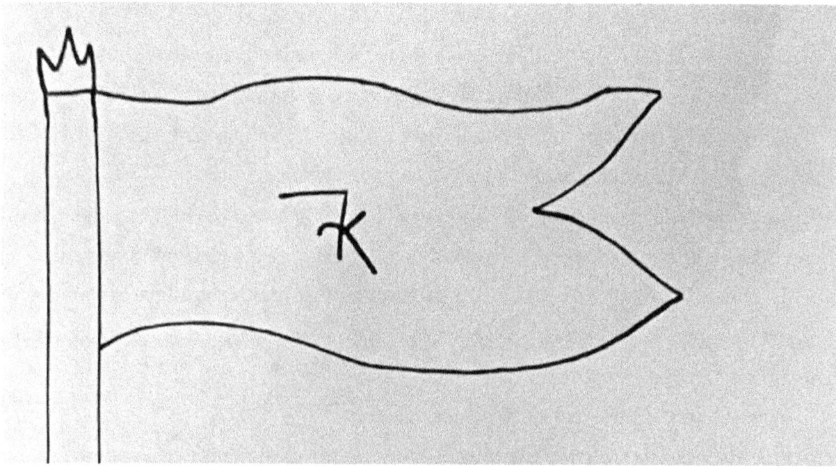

Guards on each side of the doors pushed the heavy glass open for the two, revealing a long hallway. After they walked in, the doors closed softly behind them. The hallway was bright, but there was no source of light anywhere in sight. The special glass seemed to create its own natural light. Mary followed Noah, walking down a green carpet that led to a pair of doors larger than the others around.

"This place is gorgeous." Mary spoke softly and placed a hand on the ice-cold wall next to her.

"Thank you. Not many people who have been here before appreciate the unbreakable crystal glass walls of Tay."

"Crystal? Where do you find this much?"

"There are over four thousand crystal caves here in Lotogettar. One being in the Hillshy Forest and eleven more in the mountains behind the castle."

They neared the doors at the end and the guards on the sides pushed them open. A huge open room was revealed. Noah walked ahead with Mary following slowly behind.

There wasn't much around besides two crystal thrones against the wall. Sitting upon the thrones were the King and Queen of Tay.

The king was a tall slender figure with brown hair that flowed just above his shoulders and green piercing eyes. He wore a thin green tunic with brown pants and a white silk cape. On top of his head was a crystal crown with blue rubies embedded into the several five-inch points.

The queen was different. She had a petite figure and had long golden locks and eyes like her son's. She wore an elegant white dress with golden threaded flower designs down the sides swirling at the bottom. A white cape hung loosely around her, covering her arms but not her hands that sported a bright crystal ring identical to her husbands. The crown on top of her head was a circlet with seven blue rubies that dangled loosely. A soft smile erupted on their faces as they saw their son. Their eyes drifted over to Mary and grew interested, wondering who this strange girl was. Noah walked forward and kneeled before the neanimorphic couple.

The king raised an eyebrow and spoke in a deep smooth voice.

"*Lye fin…iyeh mel sho a sallien mes sho wentail yeh teneete ly.*" (My son…I have told you a million times you do not have to kneel to me).

"*Tar. Mora.*" (Right. Sorry) Noah stood back up.

"*Laya ji shor shana?*" (Who is your friend?) The king nodded towards Mary.

"*Esa ji Mary—*" (This is Mary—)

Before Noah could continue his rant, the king interrupted him, speaking calmly and looking Mary in the eyes.

"Bea Mary yar gela sho rim?"

Mary looked him back in the eyes. Completely clueless of what he told her.

"Father…she does not speak our language…I do not believe she is from here."

"Oh…forgive me, Lady Mary. Where are you from?"

"I'm from New York…sir," Mary replied shyly.

The king frowned in confusion. "New York? I've never heard of that kingdom… who's your king?"

"There is no king…there's a president, though."

He looked back at her, mirroring her confused state and crossed his legs putting a finger on his chin thinking aloud.

"You have an odd accent and your clothes are quite odd as well, but other than that, you look normal except for that red hair. I've never seen such a pretty color. You only hear of red-haired people from *New Earth* in the fairy tales…."

The king and queen gasped, sharing a look and realizing where Mary was from.

"I have only heard of New Earth in the fairy tales my mother would read to me. A more developed place than Lotogettar. This can't be possible unless…the prophecy!" the king mumbled to his queen before looking back at Mary. "Lady Mary…I am sorry to be blunt, but you are not from here…and I would have no idea how to send you back to your world."

Mary frowned, still very confused. How could she be in a whole other world?

The king continued. "But I welcome you to Tay Kingdom. I am King Gregory Tay and this is Queen Wendy."

A small smile replaced her frown. For some reason, she already felt at home even if she had no idea where she was.

"It's nice to meet you, Mr. and Mrs. Tay."

"Please call us Gregory and Wendy. A friend of our son is a friend of ours," the queen said with a welcoming smile. "With all settled…Noah, will you please get Mary settled in a room. I will send a maid."

Noah nodded and motioned for Mary to follow him. Leaving Gregory and Wendy to their thoughts. They sighed contently. Happy that their son had finally made a friend. But also very confused about the whole situation.

***

"And so the wizard…."

Noah's voice drifted off as they came to a white wooden door identical to all the other doors in the castle except for the front main ones.

"This shall be your room. My room is just next door, so if you're in trouble or need me, you'll know where to find me. I shall get you in two hours for lunch. See you then."

He left to his room just next door like he said, leaving Mary alone.

Hesitantly she opened the door and closed it behind her slowly. Turning around, she gasped, seeing the huge room. It was way bigger than hers back home.

The walls glistened and a painting of a dragon hung right on the side. In the center was a queen-size mattress with light blue bed sheets and long white curtains that hung from the wooden bedpost.

A cool breeze blew past Mary, making her shiver. She looked towards an open balcony with more curtains around it that moved with the wind. Mary softly pushed the light curtains out of the way, walking out into the open and gaped at the sight before her. The large hills with snow covering the tops sat peacefully as clouds slowly rolled by. Mary leaned on the cold smooth railing with her head in her hands gazing out at the beauty that Lotogettar held.

"Do you still believe that this is all but a dream?" someone said.

Mary smiled, looking over to Noah who was on his own balcony.

"It's all too real to be a dream. I don't know what to believe anymore," she replied and walked back into her room.

Knock! Knock!

Mary went over to her door, wondering who that could be. Opening it, she peeked her head out to see a woman with long brown hair wearing a silk green dress. Opening the door wider, the women walked in holding a silver platter that held a towel and a pitcher of water. The lady smiled warmly at Mary and spoke softly.

"Hiled Bea Mary lye nual ji Jenna. I shenil bik shor maiden roe il lid il sho menda ter." (Hello, Lady Mary. My name is Jenna. I will be your maid for as long as you stay here.)

Mary looked at her with a sincere smile.

"I don't understand…I'm sorry."

Jenna sent her a soft smile, repeating what she said in English.

"Here let me get that for you."

Mary reached out to grab the tray before Jenna reared back, not letting her touch it.

"Oh no! Lady Mary, I cannot make you do that—"

"I insist." Mary grabbed the tray and placed it down on the bed.

"Oh alright…come along, then. Let's get you bathed."

After Mary washed all the mud and dirt from her hair and body, Jenna handed her a light blue dress. The silk material had long sleeves with golden swirls and flowers that covered half the bottom just like Wendy's dress.

"I hope you're not mad, but we threw away your old dress. The mud stained it."

"No, it's fine…this dress is way more gorgeous."

It really was with the long flowy sleeves and skirt that held tiny crystals embedded into it. This dress outshined the old dress that Mary had worn too many times.

"Well, I'm glad it is to your liking. While you were bathing, Noah dropped it off saying it would match with your beautiful red hair."

Jenna left, leaving Mary to her thoughts. She plopped down on the comfy bed wearing a bright smile.

"Lotogettar…."

Chapter Three

Time went by as Mary lay on her bed. She was about to doze off when a loud knock from the other side of the door sounded, causing her to jolt out of her tired state. Not tired anymore Mary was a little upset at being fully woken from almost taking the nap she needed badly. Another knock sounded as she walked over to the door. The blond-haired prince came into view when Mary swung the door open. His fist was held up, ready to knock again, but he brought it down once he spotted Mary.

"Hello Lady Mary! Sorry if I woke you. You look quite tired."

"You didn't wake me, but please just call me Mary."

Noah looked stunned at her request. "But that would be disrespectful," he said

"Were friends now…right?" Mary asked, raising an eyebrow

"Yes. Of course we are."

"Well, where I'm from we call each other by our names. So I'll call you just Noah and you call me just Mary."

"Well, then, just Mary you can call me just Noah,." he joked horribly and continued. "I have come to collect you for lunch."

He held out an arm, interlocked it with Mary's and pulled her through the maze-like castle all the while going on and on blabbering about the wizard he was so fascinated by.

They shortly arrived at the dining room. Noah pulled a chair out for Mary to sit at the long wooden table.

"Thank you."

He pushed her chair back in and sat down across from her. The queen soon strolled in accompanied by two guards who stopped by the doors to guard them. Wendy smiled at the two sitting down at the end of the table as the servers came out holding plates and bowls of salad in their grasps. They placed silverware and plates filled with lettuce, tomatoes, and nuts in front of the three and an empty seat that awaited the king. Mary's stomach rumbled only now realizing how hungry she was, and she went to grab her fork before stopping. Noah and Wendy hadn't lifted their hands from their laps, not touching their plates yet. They must have been waiting for the king.

Mary thought correctly as the king walked in gracefully. He sat down and began eating, everyone following suit. Lifting her fork Mary poked the salad around inspecting it. What if this were a trap and this food was…. poisoned? She trusted them too quickly.

Shaking off her paranoia, Mary took a bite of the dressing-covered lettuce. It was fine, perfect even. Her eyes widened at how delectable the meal was. Her mother never cooked like this before, but Mary would never admit this to her.

"So, Mary…how are you liking Tay Kingdom so far," Gregory asked.

"I love it here. This castle is so beautiful."

She wiped her mouth with her wrist.

"You did get a napkin right?" Noah questioned.

"Sorry…it's a habit." Mary bashfully blushed.

"But no doubt you are right. You are…very beautiful—I-I mean it's beautiful…the castle." Noah stumbled over his words as his face turned red. Mary looked back down at her plate to hide her blush; Noah doing the same continued to eat.

"Why don't you show Mary around? You have…permission to go to the village," Gregory suddenly suggested, hesitating a bit about letting Noah go to the village.

Noah nodded with a bright smile still slightly blushing and turned to Mary. "Would you like to see the village? It's truly a great place!"

"I'd love to!"

Her eyes sparkled with joy. Noah stood up, walking over to Mary's side. She finished her last bite and pushed her chair back a bit about to stand up before Noah stopped her.

"Wait! Don't stand up."

Noah rushed to her side lending her an arm to walk her out.

"Why couldn't I stand up myself?"

"It would be disrespectful for me to let a fair lady like yourself stand up from a chair without a prince to help her."

Gregory and Wendy sat in tranquility, watching the two leave with smiles upon their faces.

"Shall we tell her of the prophecy?"

"Not yet…but soon."

***

Noah led Mary deep into the castle, soon finding themselves at a dead end. On the wall hung a large painting of a town glowing with red and orange flames and a dragon flying high above. Mary looked at it with wonder.

Noah gripped the side of the painting pulling it to the side away from Mary's view. A hidden tunnel made of stones was revealed. Moss was buried in the cracks and cobwebs hung loosely from the top.

"It's just through here."

He grabbed her hand pulling her off through the long dark tunnel. Mary managed to dodge each cobweb that came in her way as they ran through, soon coming to the end of the tunnel.

"I go through here every chance I get, but we must be quiet," Noah whispered.

He slowly removed what seemed to be an old painting leading into a small attic filled with cobwebs and dust. He quietly moved from the cramped tunnel into the old room, Mary following.

Mary moved about the room searching for a way out. Artifacts, burned-out candlewicks, and old paintings were scattered about. Turning back to Noah, she saw he was gazing at a black and white painting, almost in a daydream. The painting was of a girl and boy in a field. Snow surrounded them as the girl lay in the boy's arms staring up at him. Though they held no emotion, you could tell they were in love.

"Someday that is going to be me and my beloved," he said lovingly.

Mary laughed softly at how badly he desired something that could be so heartbreaking in the end. She turned around and continued looking for a way out when a trap door came into view. Bending down she began to lift it.

Creak…

"*Shh!*" Noah exclaimed as the wooden door creaked loudly. He rushed over and quietly lowered the door from Mary's grip.

"Why do we have to be so quiet?" Mary asked in a hushed tone.

"Because right below us is an antique shop but this attic hasn't been used in a long time and if people hear us, they will come up here and find the tunnel to the castle, and I will get in so much trouble."

"Then how do we get out of here? I really don't like spiders." Mary shuddered a bit, swiping a cobweb that almost blew in her face. A childish smirk fell on Noah's face and he tickled the back of her neck with his hand to imitate a spider.

"*AH!*"

His eyes widened, not expecting her to scream out and quickly shushed her, clasping a hand over her mouth and pulling her into his chest. Mary pushed him away, glaring daggers at him. She didn't look pleased.

"Right, sorry…this way."

He led her to the corner of the room moving a box to show a hole broken out in the wall and leading outside, big enough to fit a person.

"Ladies first."

Mary eagerly peeked her head out checking around their surroundings. She wanted to get out of there as soon as possible. Looking down, she saw a small ledge that was only two inches wide and wrapped around the building. Mary struggled a bit with her dress putting one foot out, the other following and making her way out onto the thin ledge. She slowly moved her feet along and gripped the roof. She looked down, which was a huge mistake, seeing the long drop below. Mary looked back seeing Noah climb out with ease next to her.

"Are you alright?" he asked.

"Not really…no. I've never been in a position like this before." Mary tensed with fear. Noah laughed a little.

"Do not worry It's just a *little* drop."

Mary scoffed at his exaggeration of the word *little*.

"You're going to follow after me. Okay? If you don't you could possibly fall to your death," he said seriously, making Mary's anxiety rise higher.

"Thank you. That makes me feel *so* much better."

Noah placed a hand on Mary's shoulder sending her a reassuring smile and leapt agilely across the alleyway down below and landing on a lower roof.

"Come on, Mary…just like I did."

Turning to meet his soft blue eyes, Mary closed her green ones, letting go of the roof, and jumped across. All fear seemed to go away until she landed. Her eyes widened in fear as her foot got caught in a crack. She panicked and stumbled backwards. Mary was so terrified. Not even a single peep could be let out as her breath hitched in her throat. She squeezed her eyes shut once more waiting to hit the hard cold stone below.

But it never came when a pair of two strong arms wrapped around her waist, hauling her back up to safety. Mary opened her eyes to be met with a terrified Noah, holding her tightly in his arms, scared that if he let go she would fall again.

All Mary could manage to speak out was "Thank you…."

Noah gently swiped his thumb across her cheek wiping away the tear that she didn't even know was there.

"Please never do that to me again. I cannot lose my only friend here," he whispered in her ear, hugging her tightly.

"You won't lose me. I promise."

"Let's get down from here."

Mary nodded, shaking with fear, and followed him across the roof. They climbed down a wooden ladder, Mary relieved to place her feet on the ground. Looking around she noticed there weren't any people around besides an elderly couple. Noah grabbed her hand and pulled her along down the street past cobblestone structures.

"Why is nobody around?" Mary asked, trying to keep up with him.

"This part of town is the home to everyone. Nobody stays home during the day."

"Then why did we have to be quiet? And why did you make me take that jump!" Mary asked in anger.

"Mr. Norten, who is the owner of the antique shop, is the only one that stays home all day…and I don't think he would appreciate the Prince of Tay sneaking through a tunnel that leads into his home."

Noah came to a halt as Mary rammed into his back. Stepping back she rubbed her head in pain.

"A warning would be nice next time."

"Sorry."

"It's fine—"

Forgetting all about the near-death experience, a bright smile erupted on her face as she watched the people dance about to the sounds of a flute playing as more instruments joined in. As Mary and Noah strolled through the crowd, of young cheerful men and women a few kids ran past, giggling with jubilant smiles.

"Ahhh! It's the prince!"

A high-pitched squeal came from a group of girls across the street. Noah gave them a short wink as they walked past. Mary chuckled as they began to fight over which one of them he winked at.

Finding themselves in front of where people danced around, Noah turned to Mary holding out his hand.

"May I have this dance?"

"You may…though I'm not a very good dancer." She hesitantly placed her hand in his.

"Do not fret. Follow my lead."

A few glares were thrown at them as Noah tugged Mary in between people, shoving them slightly and made it to the middle of the dancing crowd. The girls from before that were heard fawning over Noah, wore envious looks upon their makeup-caked faces, watching the two begin to dance. Mary listened to the strange, fast upbeat music that she never heard before and tried to follow along with Noah's steps. Unexpectedly Noah spun her around and pulled her back in closely. With big smiles on their faces they continued happily dancing.

"You know I never asked you…what year is it?" Mary shouted over the loud music

"It's 1489!"

"1489…," she repeated Noah's words with a stunned look. Losing focus she suddenly stepped on his toes and fell backwards for the third time that day. Almost inches away from the ground Noah spun her back up into a dip and then stood straight back up with Mary still trapped in his arms.

"I think that's enough dancing for now."

"I think so too."

Noah pulled Mary off to the side and walked down a stone pathway with his arm still perched around her waist. They walked past different shops and more music continued to play in the background.

"Come on, I want to take you to my favorite bakery. It's just around the corner." Noah spoke with ecstasy and sped his pace up.

Mary caught a whiff of the sweet smell of pastries as they grew closer. Just before they turned the corner, a leg suddenly interlocked with Noah's and tripped him to the ground into a puddle of mud. Laughter erupted from the mouths of four boys.

"Oh…so sorry for that *shor quental*," (Your Highness) one mocked.

Mary sent the boy a dirty look and leaned down to Noah's side. She grabbed his muddy hands as he leaned on his knees getting back up. The expression on Noah's face was unreadable to Mary. She could not tell if he was furious or scared.

"The prince needs the help of a woman to get back up, pathetic," another spat, causing another eruption of laughter to come forth from their throats.

Mary grew angry and stepped in front of the guy who tripped him. She was intimidated a bit by his lanky height but refused to back off.

"Hello there, sweetheart. It is a real man you want to hang out with and not that *Quagerfuk*," the boy said and picked Mary's hand up kissing it gently.

Disgusted, Mary pulled her hand away and reared it back, slapping him in the face.

The boy gasped, taking a step back dumbfounded. He rubbed the stinging red mark on his cheek. Mary put her arms up ready to block a hit as the boy stepped forward. He grabbed her elbows and furiously shouted, "How dare you! You *whore*."

"Don't touch her!" Noah yelled and punched the boy in the face. He staggered back and pushed Mary into the prince's arms.

"Mary, are you alright?" Noah asked, glancing down at her worriedly.

"Yes."

Noah pushed Mary behind him protectively watching the four boys puff up their chests, ready to fight the prince. They did not care that he was the prince. These four boys did not care about anyone really. They were a small group that would gang up on anyone they did not like, including the prince.

The boy Noah punched started forward and raised his fists back and welted Noah in the eye. Mary grabbed his shoulders to steady his balance as he stumbled back holding his eye in pain. Noah groaned, growing dizzy a bit. Once he got back his consciousness he grabbed Mary's hand and quickly took off running down a nearby alleyway.

"GET BACK HERE, YOU COWARDS!" the boy yelled and began running after them followed by his friends.

Mary stumbled over her dress and let go of Noah's hand trying to keep up with him.

"Come on, Mary, faster!"

"I'm trying!"

Mary gripped her dress, holding it up past her feet so she did not trip. Noah slowed his pace and fell back to Mary's side, re-grabbed her hand, holding it tightly in his and tugged her along. They ran as fast as they could, Mary effortlessly keeping up with Noah's long legs.

The two turned down another alleyway and suddenly came to a halt. Facing an eight-foot stone wall.

"Give me your foot," Noah said, getting down on one knee and interlocking his hands together.

Mary placed her small foot on his hands and jumped a bit grabbing the top of the wall as Noah pushed her up and over it. She jumped to the grassy ground, and only a second later Noah hopped over, landing next to her. The faint noise of one of the boys shouting could be heard. "Where did they go!?"

Noah let out a shaky sigh and turned to Mary.

"Please do not let my father or mother know that just happened," he breathed out.

"I won't." Mary nodded.

"It is getting late." Noah gestured to the sun that began to set on the horizon and continued, "We should probably head back."

Mary nodded once more and Noah grabbed her hand, feeling a slight tingle in his chest as he did and headed in the direction of his home.

***

Arriving back to the castle late, they missed dinner. But that did not matter to Noah. he did not want to sit with his parents and hear them ask constant questions about what happened to his now bruised eye.

Mary and Noah both separated at their rooms. A euphoric feeling ran through their bodies as they both fell down on their beds. Despite being chased by a gang and possibly could have faced worse than a beating, that could not ruin everything else that happened before when they were together dancing and in each other's arms.

Moments later Jenna came knocking on Mary's door, breaking her out from her happy state of mind, daydream. She came in with a small platter of food and placed it beside Mary before heading off. Mary looked down at the food, which was just one small turkey leg that included a crystal chalice filled with wine to drink.

A soft knock was heard at the door.

"Come in!" Mary yelled, taking a bite of turkey.

Noah peeked his head in, wearing a dimpled smile.

"Could I join you?"

"Yeah, come in."

She watched as he opened the door more and walked in sitting on the hard floor next to her bed. She saw his black eye as he looked up to her with a smile. It was worse than before. His eye seemed to stick shut and grow puffy and a dark shade of purple.

"You know you can sit on the bed next to me."

"Mary, it would be quite rude for a man to sit on a lady's bed without courting her," Noah explained with a smirk. "Unless that is…if you want me to court you. Courting means marriage if you did not already know—"

Mary cut him off with a scoff as a blush reached her cheeks. "No! I mean, wouldn't it be rude to let a prince sit on the floor."

"Well…I guess you're right," Noah replied as the same red tint appeared on his face. He hesitated before awkwardly sitting next to her.

"Relax. I don't bite," Mary replied jokingly.

"That's what the last girl said."

"What?"

"Nothing… thank you for being so kind to me. You've been my first real friend here. Well… besides my family." He took a sip of wine from his chalice.

"What do you mean. You don't have any friends?"

"Well…." Noah laughed sadly and gestured to his black eye, and continued. "Most of the boy's my age are not so kind. They think I am stuck up and others just want to be my friend because I am—"

"The prince."

"Yeah and I have never had a friend that is a girl because they are usually jumping at me, desperate for my attention." He ended the conversation there with a sad smile.

As they finished their meals, Noah noticed Mary didn't touch her wine.

"You haven't had any of your wine."

"I've never had wine before. My mom always says that I should not drink it till I get in my forties." She laughed a bit thinking of when her mom would say wine is for when you lived forty years and had children.

"Forty! I have been drinking wine since I was twelve years old." He then continued rolling his eyes. "I'm only allowed one glass a week, though, since I am only eighteen. Well then, go on and try it."

Holding the cup between her nimble fingers she looked down at the blood red liquid and put her nose to the rim smelling the bittersweet aroma. Taking a small sip her face contorted with disgust coughing at the sharp pungent taste.

Noah looked offended at this. "Do you not like it?"

"No…no. I'm just not used to the taste." She hid her disgusted face.

"You get used to it after a while. Hey I—"

Jenna walked in before he could finish.

"Oh! There you are. I was wondering why you were not in your room. Here let me get those. It is getting quite late. I suggest you two get some sleep."

She grabbed their plates, then left them alone again.

Walking with Noah to the door Mary spoke softly. "Thank you for today. I had fun earlier."

"You're welcome. I'm glad you enjoyed everything. I shall retire to my chambers. I will see you in the morning."

Mary yawned tiredly and slumped in her bed covering herself with the warm silk blankets. The moon glowed through the curtain that blew slightly in the wind. Closing her eyes Mary thought of her mother, aunt, and Max, wondering when she would go back and see them again. Soon she was sent into a REM-like state awaiting the next morning.

Chapter Four

Ashes, with little sparks of fire flew through the sky! The sound of glass crunching beneath Mary's feet and suddenly she was pulled out of the way followed by someone yelling.

"Look out!"

Sent into panic she jolted awake, sitting upright in bed. Mary wiped away a bead of sweat on her forehead, breathing heavily. She wondered why all of a sudden she had a new dream. Closing her eyes again, the sparkling flames flashed vividly in her eyes. Upon opening them again she sighed, trying to ignore the tense feeling she held. Standing up out of bed, she stretched out and walked over to her balcony, leaning on the cold railing like she did yesterday and peered out at the vast mountains.

"Good morning, Mary," Noah's voice sounded.

Looking over to him, his hair was tousled about. He stretched his arms out, giving Mary a short smile.

"Good morning."

"How did you—"

"Lady Mary! Where are you?"

Jenna shouted from Mary's room, interrupting Noah.

"Better not keep Jenna waiting…she can be quite impatient at times. I shall see you at breakfast."

After breakfast Noah grabbed Mary's hand, tugging her out of the room immediately after she finished her last bite. He ran with her down many hallways and up many stairs coming to the tallest point of the castle. They walked out to a balcony larger than the ones connected to their rooms. The balcony overlooked the misty mountains. Mary gawked at the sight. The vast snowy hills seemed a lot closer from this part of the castle, almost towering over them.

"Do you see it?" Noah asked with a smirk.

"See what?" Mary looked at him confused.

"There."

He pointed to a specific part of the mountain. Squinting her eyes, she saw a cave with silver bars caging something in. Looking closer a puff of smoke blew out through the bars.

"What's in there?" Mary asked intrigued.

"You would never believe me if I told you." Noah turned around and began to walk back inside and continued. "Follow me."

Mary walked behind, speeding up a bit trying to keep up with his long strides.

They walked down a hallway leading up to a pair of large green stained-glass doors. Noah opened the doors, letting Mary pass first. The room was a wide gallery of paintings and statues. At the end of the room was a mystery.

A green drape hung up hiding something. Slowly walking down the rug planted in the middle, Mary surveyed the many paintings leading up the walls to the turret ceiling painted with warriors fighting dragons.

She looked back down at a large painting of Gregory, Wendy, Noah, and a boy a few years older than him that looked exactly like Gregory. They all wore intimidating looks with their crowns and circlets lying powerfully on their heads.

"Who's that?"

Mary pointed to the boy next to Noah. A sad smile appeared on Noah's face as he replied, "That's my brother. Though I haven't seen him in two years because he has been with his wife in Plake kingdom."

He continued on pulling her over to a large map of all kingdoms in Lotogettar. There were five kingdoms painted each in different colors of red, green, blue, purple, and black.

"The map of Lotogettar…. Right there is"—pointing to the purple section—"the Carone Kingdom. The rulers King Ivan and Queen Jolean have been our only enemies over the past few years."

He then pointed to the blue one.

"There is the Plake Kingdom. The ruler is King Jack III. His wife had died just a few years ago. My brother Elliot married his daughter Amandria, and then there is the Itowana Kingdom, then the Fenter Kingdom…and lastly is Caesar Kingdom. Home to my uncle King John Caesar and cousin Alexander. My mother's brother is not the nicest man. I feel bad for my cousin. We used to be such good friends. Anyways! Let us move on. There are many more paintings and ancient artifacts I would love to show you."

Mary nodded and followed slowly along until Noah stopped and turned to her with a serious face asking her the question that had been bugging him since she arrived.

"So it is true. You really aren't from here, are you?"

"I guess not."

Mary frowned as the sudden random thought of her mother came to mind. She missed Rose and felt horrible for running away like that. Would she ever go home? The last words she told her mother were *I hate you.*

Rose already lost her husband and now her daughter. The poor woman would blame herself and be in pain till she died. A tear fell from her eye at the thoughts that crowded her mind.

"Are you alright?" Noah asked.

"I'm fine...."

Before she could peep out another word, Noah softly wiped the single tear away.

"You're not...you're crying. Please don't cry or then I'll cry. It pains me to see you upset."

Mary grew confused for a second. *Why would it pain him?* She quickly forgot the thought and removed his hand from her face.

"Sorry, I don't mean to...I just miss my home." She wiped away the other tears that fell. "Well, then. Let's move on," Mary said with a fake smile plastered on her face and walked past Noah to look around more.

Walking up to a bunch of swords and armor hung on the wall, she looked at it confused. All of them were half melted or burnt by something.

"What did this...a dragon?" she joked, meeting Noah's eyes.

He smiled and stood next to her. "Indeed." He gazed at the fighting equipment with fascination.

"You're serious? There are...dragons here."

"Of course there are! Though not many roam the land of Lotogettar anymore. Most flew north, going extinct or—don't do that!" He suddenly panicked and pulled her hands away as she reached out to touch the tip of the burnt metal sword.

"You cannot touch armor or weapons that have seen battle with a dragon. A deadly power overtakes the equipment after fighting these beasts...if you would have touched that you would die immediately."

He grabbed her hand, holding it to his chest, afraid she would try to touch the metal blades again.

Pulling her away from the lethal equipment Noah brought her over to a small velvet green box. Upon opening the small case sat neatly in the middle were two pairs of gloves. They were thin and made of crystals made to fit the hand of a man.

"These gloves were given to us by Olteg the wizard of Velga. We call them *the gloves of Velga*. They were made to prevent death…or something like that…he said they were to be used sometime in the future for something big that was to happen."

"There are wizards here as well?"

"Yes…well only the one nobody else besides Olteg himself knows if there are others like him."

"So then—"

The door creaked before Mary could continue.

"Your Highness, the king wishes to meet with you in the library," a guard said, walking up to them and bowing as he spoke.

Noah sighed. "Alright. Tell him I will be there in a minute."

The guard bowed once more and left the room.

"I leave you here. I will send Jenna to help you find your way back to your room… and, whatever you do…do not look behind that curtain," he said, watching her carefully inspect the curtain that draped at the end of the room.

"Why not…?"

Her words faltered, seeing the blond prince gone from sight. She turned back to the curtain. With Noah now gone she did what he told her not to.

Her curiosity peeking through, she stepped forward, walking closer and hesitantly gripped the side of the silk sheet between her fingers. Slowly moving the sheet aside enough to see inside, she gasped in fear.

The big behemoth blue-and-green scaly heads of dragons were hung on the wall above. Their auburn-colored eyes peered back at her. Before she could see any more the door creaked open once more. Mary quickly jumped back. Dropping the drape, she turned around to see Jenna.

"Come along, dear. Noah asked me to bring you back to your room."

***

Noah strolled into the library, seeing his dad leaning back in his chair and staring off in thought as his crown sat on the table in front of him.

"Father…you wanted to see me?" Noah said, breaking his father's trance.

"Ah…there you are, son. *Telio ly.*" (Follow me.) Gregory spoke smoothly and stood up, disappearing behind some bookshelves.

Noah peered around the huge room. He hadn't been here since his brother left. He laughed at the thought of when he and his brother would always get yelled at for sitting on the wooden railing on the second floor, jumping on top of the large bookshelves and almost knocking them over as if it were some game.

"Are you coming!" Gregory yelled out.

"Yes, Father!"

Quickly he followed after his father, disappearing through the maze of bookshelves. He was led to a dead end where he met his father.

"Why did you bring me all the way back here?"

"It's time you know the truth."

Gregory knocked twice on the wall, blowing a soft breath towards it. Noah laughed and looked at him as if he were a fool.

"Father what—"

Just then the wall pushed in. A white mist was sent out from the sides.

"How did you do that! Do you hold powers within you?"

Gregory chuckled at the bewildered boy and pushed open the secret door, walking in. Noah sped in after his father and paused peering around the room. It was not big. Nor was it small.

A table was sat in the middle, large enough to fit thirty people. A map of Lotogettar was engraved into the white wood.

"Father, please answer my question!" Noah begged, looking back at Gregory.

"That wizard…Olteg…he helped build these walls placing magic within them. I do not hold any power." He grabbed a book from a bookshelf in the corner as he continued to speak. "This is where I meet with kings from other lands to discuss alliances and warfare. Someday you will use this room when you are king. Someday you will have to learn things others do not get to know…and some days are sooner than others," Gregory explained as he glided his finger across the thin paper looking for something. "Ah…here it is."

He slid the book over to his son who was now seated in a chair. Noah peered down at the book cluelessly.

"Well, go on, then…read the middle."

Looking at a cursive font, Noah read aloud:

"The prophecy of Tay…A king shall rise and the world will be at peace for a long time… but not before great destruction and a good deal of loved ones shall perish. It will all begin in

the evening when the girl like no other arrives. But if the king of cruelty plays out his way… the girl will suffer a great deal of agony and harsh punishment will rise onto the innocent."

Noah hesitated before speaking once more, hoping what he said next would not be true.

"Please tell me Mary is not a part of this."

Gregory sighed. "Yes…I am sure you have suspected she wasn't from here. The prophecy shall be fulfilled sooner than I thought. Your uncle is to be here in a couple of days. He is the cruel king they speak of and we cannot let him find out about Mary. Though at some point he will… I just hope it's later than sooner," Gregory said, growing stressed.

"Who are *'they'*…who wrote this? How do we know it is even real?"

"My father had tried many times to figure out who wrote this but till this day no one knows…and it is very real," Gregory stated.

Noah grew worried for Mary's safety. "Are you sure this is about Mary?"

"Do you know of any other redheads that walk the lands of Lotogettar?"

Chapter Five

Four days had passed since Mary arrived in Lotogettar. This place was much more different than back home in New York. There were no cars, no sodas, or her favorite style in music, rock and roll. Everything here was different…a good difference. Over the past days, Mary grew closer to the royal family. Wendy and Gregory treated her like the daughter they never had. Though Noah was now a close friend, Mary felt something else when she was around him but was completely blind to whatever it was.

Today Noah had been acting different and protective towards her and had been very adamant about her staying by his side wherever he went. Mary grew more and more annoyed by the second at his behavior. The two were currently out on the balcony viewing the sun slowly disappearing behind the mountains.

"Noah, what's wrong?"

"Nothing's wrong." He spoke obliviously to what she was implying.

"You have been tense about something all day."

Noah huffed stubbornly at her words. "My uncle and cousin are to arrive any minute."

"What does that have to do with you being so controlling today?"

"I'm sorry…it is just that my uncle could arrive at any time and I had to be ready to hide you and—"

"Why would you have to hide me?" Mary asked, confused.

Placing both of his hands gently on her shoulders he began to speak in a serious manner.

"As I told you before…my uncle is not a nice man. If he finds out about you, then he will use the prophecy against you—" His eyes widened as he stopped himself from continuing and began to walk off. "I've said too much."

"Noah, what are you talking about?" Mary caught his arm to stop him.

"It's just an old prophecy, but I can't tell you any more about it," he replied.

"Why not? You said he would use the prophecy against me. What is this prophecy? Am I a part of it?" she questioned.

He grabbed ahold of her hands softly and pulled her in close. As he spoke his warm breath gently hit her face. For a second she almost could have sworn his eyes flickered down towards her lips.

"I cannot tell you yet, but soon I will. I promise."

Looking up into his blue eyes, she was lost in thought. She ignored the alluring pull he gave off and asked the question that had been bugging her all week.

"Will I ever go home?"

"I do not know. But there is no need to worry…*Lye lunda*." Noah pulled her into a hug. Mary hugged him back breathing in his scent of mahogany wood.

"What does that mean… '*Lye lunda*'?" she asked as he placed his head on top of hers.

"It means—"

"Your Highness! King John Caesar has arrived," a guard interrupted, coming towards the two.

Noah released her, stepping back. "I leave you here, Mary. I shall see you in the morning."

***

Noah walked his way down to the dining room. He swung the doors open, wearing an intimidating look as he met eyes with his uncle. The King of Caesars Kingdom sat at the far end of the table with his son Alexander across from his parents. John was an older, fatter man with the same eyes and hair as his sister Wendy. There was nothing special about him. He always thought too highly of himself just because he was *a* king.

Alexander was different. He looked almost like Noah with the same blond hair and blue eyes but with a stronger, taller figure. Alexander's attitude changed over the years. He hid under a mask, never expressing his true feelings, acting cruel to others just like his father.

Noah gave the Caesars a short nod and sat down in the middle of the table. There was an uncomfortable silence until the servers brought out the giant turkey platter. Before they could leave, Noah called one over.

"Cado yeh kinaen film denlan te bea Mary's lendi." (please have someone bring dinner to Lady Mary's room.)

"Farnose Shor quelintail" (Of course, Your Highness.)

The server replied before sending off a maid to bring Mary dinner.

The table grew quiet again as everyone but John ate. For a second Noah felt eyes burning into the side of his head and looked up to see his uncle eyeing him suspiciously.

"Is something the matter?"

John raised an eyebrow. "Nothing's wrong…just suspicious is all."

His uncle had always been an ignorant distrustful man. Noah scoffed a bit and turned to his father.

"Jala! Satiy yeh I wean darno?" (Father? what have I done wrong?) he complained.

Gregory glanced at his son, then looked John directly in the eyes.

"Wentail kitan fin…shor pana ji vusa a inla ston." (Do not worry, son. Your uncle is just a foolish man).

"Oh come on…speak man's language! You can, you know. We're all family here, we have nothing to hide…that is, unless you are hiding something," John said and began to poke his fork around in his meal moving the food side to side as if to search for something.

"Are you implying that my son has ordered someone to poison your meal?"

Noah scoffed at his father's words and turned to his uncle.

"If I were to kill you, I would not have someone do it for me…let alone use poison… it shows *weakness.*" He spoke sarcastically, mocking the way John kills his enemies.

Bang!

"Don't you dare use that tone with me, boy!" John shouted, pounding his fist on the table like a child. Noah laughed at his pathetic behavior.

"Do not speak to my son like that—"

"ENOUGH!"

Wendy's voice rose over her husband's. All the men at the table quieted down immediately as Alexander looked on in silence. It frightened them a bit to hear her scream as she was usually a tranquil person.

"I think I will go eat in my room," John said, breaking the tension and took off out of the room with his plate.

"I think I will go as well." Alexander spoke up for the first time. He wore an almost snobbish look on his face as he followed after his father. Wendy sighed, pinching the bridge of her nose and scolded the two. "Could you please try to get along with my brother…? Both of you."

***

A loud chirping bird woke Mary. It reminded her of the old obnoxious alarm clock at home. She sighed getting up out of bed and walking barefoot along the cold floor. Opening and closing her door quietly she stood there in the hallway still in her silk blue nightgown.

Mary waited for Noah who told her to wake up earlier so they could have breakfast together, saying he didn't want to make her eat alone. Noah suddenly popped up in front of her scaring her a bit.

"You're still in your nightclothes?"

Mary yawned before she could reply. "And you're already wide awake and dressed for the day?"

"I know what will wake you up." Noah wore a mischievous smirk. "Race you to the dining room!" He suddenly took off down the hall. Mary groaned and ran after him. She silently wished he wasn't so energetic all the time.

Running down many halls, Mary lost sight of Noah and soon got lost turning down a dead end. She turned back around going down another hall, hoping it was the right way and just as she turned down the hall.

Slam!

Chapter Six

Mary fell to the floor as she bumped into something hard. She squeezed her eyes shut waiting for the painful impact. But just before she was an inch away a pair of strong arms tightly wrapped around her waist, pulling her back up.

"I am so sorry, my lady. Are you alright?" a deep rich voice spoke.

"No…I'm sorry. I bumped into you. I wasn't really watching where I was going," Mary replied, flustered and looked up at the person who she bumped into.

It was a boy who looked just like Noah. The light from the crystal walls gleamed down on his luscious blond hair and white skin. She would be lying if she said she wasn't attracted to him.

"Say…you have a strange accent and I've never seen you around during my yearly visits here. We have never crossed paths. Are you a new maid?"

"I'm not a maid. I'm a friend of Noah's."

"A friend of Noah's…," the boy repeated, mumbling under his breath. He continued sending her a charming smile as he changed the subject.

"Well, then! Shall I see you at the ball tonight?"

Mary frowned in confusion. "I didn't know there was a ball tonight."

"Noah, never told you? How rude of him. Well, now that you know, I hope to see you there." He removed his arms from her that were still perched around Mary's waist and sent her one last charming smile. "Farewell, my lady."

The blond moved past her and turned down the other hall, disappearing from sight. Realizing she never got his name Mary ran after him.

"Wait! I never got your…name."

She finished in a low whisper, seeing he was no longer there. She sighed and went on her way, wondering why Noah never told her about the ball.

Mary arrived at the dining room almost twenty minutes late, having a hard time finding her way through the large castle.

"Mary. There you are…I was starting to get worried. What took you so long?" Noah asked with a relieved look washing over him as he watched Mary walk into the dining room. He got up from the seat and pulled out one for her.

"I got lost. This place is huge," she replied.

"That was my fault. I should not have made a race out of it."

Noah sat back down in his seat. They ate in silence until Mary spoke up remembering what she wanted to ask.

"So, I heard there was a ball tonight."

Noah choked as he took a sip of water from his chalice. "How did you find out!" he exclaimed with a short cough.

"Uh, I-I…overheard a couple of maids speaking of it," she lied.

Noah scoffed. "Foolish maids do not know when to stop gossiping."

"Why didn't you tell me?" she asked

"I am sorry. I should keep no secrets from you. I am just trying to keep you safe from—"

"Your uncle," Mary finished for him.

Noah sighed.

"I wish you could have come. If so you would have been *my* dancing partner." The two blushed at the thought of being in each other's arms. "Maybe…you can go." Noah spoke again as an idea popped into his head. "It is to be a masquerade ball after all."

***

Later that night the plan was to sneak Mary into the crowd of all the people from town who were invited to the ball. It would be hard since Mary would stand out being the only redhead, but Noah insisted she would blend right in.

Jenna had quickly thrown a dress over Mary's head as she was already late for the ball. The dress was a long royal blue ball gown. The sleeves were flowy and cut off, showing her shoulders.

"You look beautiful! Oh and here," Jenna said and handed Mary a blue silk mask that covered the top part of her face as her forest-green eyes peered through the holes. Jenna then pulled out a golden hairclip with a small butterfly engraved into it.

"That's beautiful," Mary said.

She looked at the way it shined as it reflected off the walls. Jenna smiled sadly, moving her thumb gently across the smooth clip.

"Turn around."

Mary turned around and felt two locks of her hair being pulled back and clipped jointly.

Jenna continued to speak. "It was my younger sister's. You look just like her, besides for the red hair. Her name was Christalyne. She died when she was just your age from… a deadly illness."

"I'm so sorry," Mary responded with remorse knowing what it's like to lose someone you love dearly.

"Keep it."

Mary turned around to face her, smiling kindly but shook her head. "It's a lovely gift, but I could not take something that is so valuable to you."

"It is yours now, Mary," Jenna said, pulling Mary into a tight hug as a tear escaped her eyes. "Now, let's get you to the ball." Together they ran down many halls, making it to the ballroom. "This is where I leave you. Have fun!"

Jenna gave her one last hug before walking away. Music could be heard from the other side of the grand doors as two Tay soldiers stood on either side. They opened the door for her, revealing the gallant room and releasing the music that grew louder. Walking in slowly, she stopped at the top of the wide staircase that led down into the sea of dancing people. Mary looked around and stopped, gazing at the beautiful crystal chandelier that hung high above from the ceiling.

Letting out a shaky breath, she took a step forward and began down the stairs. Mary was never one to go to big events. She was shy and uncomfortable being in large groups like this. What only made it worse was when she was halfway down the stairs and almost there, she felt a ton of eyes on her. The flat velvet blue shoes she wore finally stepped flat at the bottom of the stairs. Mary stared down at her feet with her face redder than her hair. The people took their eyes off her not caring anymore and turned back to their conversations. Relieved from the stress, Mary walked to the side of the room with fewer people and searched for Noah. Giving up she moved forward through the crowd, pushing past some people, apologizing as they sent a glare her way.

A head of blond hair came into view. Quickly Mary raced over to the boy who was standing alone and tapped his shoulder. The boy turned around and looked down at her. A small smirk appeared on his face.

"Noah, I almost could not find you. I thought you said you were wearing a blue suit…not a red one."

The boy's smirk turned into a frown.

"Don't you remember me from before?" he said almost arrogantly.

His voice sounded familiar but Mary could not seem to recollect.

"I'm not sure I know…."

The glum look that sat upon his face soon turned up right into a charming smile.

"You ran into me earlier in the morning."

The memory from that morning replayed in her head.

"Yeah, I do remember now. I never got your name, though."

"Well, then, allow me to introduce myself." He took her hand in his and kissed it lightly.

"I am Alexander, and shall I ask for your name?"

Blushing she opened her mouth about to reply before someone came running over and lightly placed a cold hand on her bare shoulder.

"Mary, there you are. I was looking everywhere for you," Noah said, placing his other hand on her forearm protectively.

"*Mary*…what a beautiful name," Alexander whispered, still holding her hand in his warm one.

Immediately Noah pulled Mary's hand from his. Alexander straightened his back and said, in an almost challenging tone and looking directly into his cousin's eyes, "Dear cousin…I was wondering what mask you hid under."

"Yeah, I was wondering the same thing about *you* nine years ago," Noah shot back, trying to antagonize him. The two glared daggers into each other's heads from under their masks as the tension rose.

"Come along, Mary. Let us go elsewhere."

Noah pulled her away from him.

"I didn't know Alexander was your cousin," Mary said as they pushed through the crowd.

"I did not know you two had already met," Noah replied with jealousy lacing his voice.

Alexander grew more aggravated watching the two walk off. He refused to give up so easily.

The song playing in the background came to an end, starting up a new one. Acting quickly, he ran towards them and jumped in front of Mary.

"Before you leave *elsewhere*…would you care to take this dance, Mary?"

He held out a hand to her, bowing. Mary took his hand, not wanting to be rude.

Noah's heart broke a bit and, seeing his sad reaction, Mary let go of Alexander's hand and took Noah's in hers, pressing a kiss to his cheek.

"Don't worry, I will dance with you next."

"Alright, enough of this! Let us hurry up before all spots are taken." Alexander pulled her away from him. He was being a bit too pushy.

Noah blushed, placing a hand to where her soft lips had touched. But that could not stop the anger and jealousy that surged through him as Alexander glanced back smirking mockingly. Stepping onto the floor where couples lined up to dance, Alexander pulled Mary in closer.

"I must warn you I'm not the best dancer, so if I step on your foot, I'm sorry."

Alexander chuckled at her words. "Just follow my lead."

They began to glide on the dance floor with the other couples until a slow waltz began to play. All the other couples were filled with comfort and joy being in each other's arms, but it was a different story with Alexander and Mary.

At first he was kind and gentle. But as soon as the song came to an end his eyes were filled with desire and control from behind his mask. Mary shifted a bit in Alexander's tight hold that was around her waist. He guided her through the crowd and to the grand staircase.

"Are you alright, Mary? You seem a bit tense."

"I-I am fine. I should probably go find Noah now. Thank you for the dance," she replied nervously, slipping out of his grip and going to move past him.

"Don't leave me so soon. The ball has only just begun. I am sure Noah is busy talking to other girls. What about another dance? Or we could go out into the gardens and get some fresh air. It is getting quite a bit stuffy in here." Alexander blocked her from moving past him each time she tried to.

"Look. I need to find Noah, so if you would please excuse me." Mary went to make a dash for it, speeding past him. Before she could get far, Alexander gripped her arm, hauling her back into his arms.

"Let go of me!" She began to panic and squirmed around in his arms trying to get him to release her from his tight grip.

"Shhh!? Please calm down. People are starting to watch!" he exclaimed in a hushed tone as onlookers looked on suspiciously at the small commotion. In a quick second someone punched him hard in the face. Alexander lost his grip and leaned over holding his face in pain and looked up making eye contact with Noah.

"What the hell is wrong with you!" Noah yelled.

He furiously pushed his cousin backwards onto the crystal flooring. Alexander immediately scrambled off the floor and yelled back, "There is nothing wrong with me!"

The music came to a stop and now everyone turned their heads to see what was happening. Alexander's voice lowered to a growl as he pointed directly at Mary. "That *whore* is the problem. She—"

Before he could finish King Gregory rushed over in fury. He pinched the backs of the two cousins' necks, making them wince in pain. Gregory motioned for the music to continue playing as he pulled the two up the stairs and slammed the heavy doors behind him.

The music went back to its slow tune, but the eyes stayed put. Mary stood there feeling sheepish looking directly back into the eyes of the onlookers. A sudden feeling of guilt washed over her. If she hadn't come, they would not be in trouble. She thought this was all her fault and broke from her frozen stance and immediately rushed up the stairs after them.

Opening the doors the king's voice boomed loudly through the halls not only scaring Mary and the two boys, but the guards as well.

"I am very disappointed in both of your actions! And you, son, have disobeyed me. I asked you one simple thing and you ignored me! I told you Mary was to not be seen at the ball, but I am sure you insisted that she come along. You have put her life in danger…your brother would never—"

"It wasn't his fault!" Mary interrupted, announcing her presence.

They all turned to her.

"Mary, please don't. It was my fault," Noah said over her, not wanting her to take the blame for his wrongdoing.

"I begged Noah to let me come along. I'm sorry."

Gregory sighed. "I am very angry with both of you and shame on you Alexander, holding a woman captive like that! You're lucky I don't lock you up in the dungeons."

Just then a rather large guy burst through the doors. Noah immediately pushed Mary behind him to hide her from his uncle's sight.

"You have gone too far this time *Tay*! How dare you lay your hands on my son."

Gregory scoffed. "Would you prefer both of our sons start a war in front of all of my kingdom and embarrass the two of us…more you. They will witness the true nature of the savages that live within the walls of Caesar's Kingdom!"

"You dare insult my kingdom!" John roared back, pointing at Gregory with an accusing finger. "Your son brought on this fight!"

Gregory Pinched the bridge of his nose to contain his anger and spoke calmly. "You did not even witness what happened. You were too busy drinking all the wine and shoving food down that big hole in your face."

John lowered his tone to a grumpy one. "Well, then. What was the real cause of this fight?"

Mary sighed and walked out from behind Noah. "I caused it."

John walked over to Mary towering over her.

"Who is this young maiden? A mere peasant from town, I suppose…no…there is something different about you." He frowned in confusion as he eyed her red hair but quickly brushed it off. "Never mind…I will let this one pass us for now." He gripped Alexander's arm and pulled him down the hallway before stopping one last time, turning to Mary. "You girl…I shall see to it that you are to attend dinner with us all tomorrow night."

Gregory sighed and turned to the two after John left. "I am very disappointed in you, Noah. You must be punished for your actions. For the rest of the night you are to go to your rooms and, Noah, I am sorry but…you are banned from going back to the village."

Noah's sad expression turned into a shocked one. "What! That's not fair. You cannot keep me locked in this castle."

"I am not putting you on lockdown. You are allowed to go anywhere else, but the village." Gregory looked at his son with guilt. "I'm sorry but you must learn." With that said, he walked back into the ballroom.

Seeing Noah's perturb reaction, Mary pulled him into a hug.

"I'm sorry I caused all this chaos."

He shook his head, hugging her back. "I should be the one apologizing. I put your life in danger."

Chapter Seven

The next day came by fast and it was almost time for Mary to join dinner with the royal family. A sudden wave of nervousness washed over her. Could it have been seeing Alexander again or his father? Both frightened her. King John eyed her with a crazed look in his eyes as if he knew her already when he did not and wanted to slaughter her. The way Alexander stared at her was different. His blue eyes were filled with such desire and need. The thought of what Alexander wanted from her scared her.

Letting out a sigh, Mary walked onto her balcony and leaned on the railing watching the sunset, like she did every night.

"What is on your mind? *Lye lunda?*" Noah asked from his balcony.

"It's nothing…but I still don't know what *lye lunda* means."

"In time you will find out." He sent her a wink before disappearing into his room.

***

Knock! Knock!

"Mary! It's me…I've come to escort you down to dinner," Noah said from the other side of the door. He sounded nervous.

Mary pulled back her hair, clipping it up with the golden clip. Rushing over to the door she opened it. Noah stood there with a lopsided grin.

"You look beautiful…*lye lunda.*"

He tilted his head slightly and grabbed her hand, kissing her knuckles.

"Thank you."

She blushed.

Noah took her arm and guided her to the dining room.

They stopped before the doors where his family was on the other side. Noah turned to Mary.

"Whatever the questions my uncle asks you. Lie."

Mary nodded and followed him in as he kept his tight grip on her arm.

They were greeted by Gregory and Wendy, though John and Alexander seemed to be late. Noah pulled out a chair in the middle of the table for Mary and sat down in the one next to her. Everyone sent each other a warm smile like any family would, but Mary could not help but feel something was off. The pessimistic feeling went away as the doors swung open.

In walked King John and his son taking long strides to their seats across the table from Gregory and Wendy.

Both were wearing the same long red velvet cloaks that glided with them.

Two of their guards followed in after them, stationing themselves in the corner of the room.

The atmosphere was tense as they ate in silence. It was quiet for a few seconds until John made a ton of noise scarfing down his food greedily.

At one point it sounded as if he were choking. A look of disgust was evident on Mary's face as she stared down at her plate, slowly losing her appetite. John stopped for a second and placed his fork down looking up from his plate at Mary.

"So…Mary, is it? My son told me about you." They all turned to him. "So sorry you had to see me so enraged like that yesterday. I am usually a nice guy." A low scoff escaped Noah's lips at his statement. Glaring at his nephew, John asked, "Do not mind if I ask but…are you from around here?"

Gregory panicked and looked to Mary hoping she would lie.

"Uh…yeah I'm from the town," Mary replied hesitantly.

John cocked an eyebrow. "Really? I've never seen anyone in Lotogettar with such beautiful red hair as yours. And your accent…it is quite different from ours."

Mary nudged Noah's foot from underneath for help, not knowing what to say.

"U-uh…she was the first to be born with red hair and as for the accent…she moved here from across seas a year ago. Turns out people from across seas are different from us."

John nodded at his lie and went back to eating. Before Noah went back to eating, he made eye contact with Alexander and smirked. The sight of a black and blue bruises sat right below his eyes.

"Gregory, I must ask…have you promised your son to anyone yet?" John asked.

Gregory looked at John with slight disgust as small bits of food flew from his mouth.

"No, I have not. As you saw with my other son…I will allow Noah to marry for love and not politics as well," he replied adamantly.

"Recently, I have come to an arrangement with the Carone Kingdom. Alexander is to be married to Princess Ladghadith Carone in twelve months." John sounded proud of his statement.

"That should be good for your kingdom," Gregory replied, taking a sip of wine.

"Why is that?"

"Caesar Kingdom might have great rulers for once."

John scoffed at his words. "What do you mean? Are you referring to me as a bad king!"

From there the two argued back and forth, growing louder by the second. They were like two dogs fighting over a sack of meat. Noah grew worried and grabbed Mary's hand from under the table.

"I sense a division soon upon our kin."

Mary placed her other hand on top of his in a comforting manner and began to whisper back.

"I'm sure everything is fine. You don't need to worry—"

SLAM!

The two jumped as John slammed his fist down on the table and rose from his seat.

"Do you mean what I think you said!?"

Gregory stood up as well and raised his voice higher.

"You are a callous man! The way you treat your people makes me sick."

"They are not people, they are slaves!" John spat back in a accusing tone and continued. "You have sent a spy to my lands, haven't you? What is this…some kind of mutiny!?"

"No, I have not!" Gregory defended.

And before he knew it, the fat man jumped onto the table, charging at Gregory. From under his cloak, he pulled out a sharp dagger. Everyone's eyes widened with shock.

The guards jumped into action to defend their king but were stopped by John's guards, fighting back and forth.

Gregory held no weapons on him but nonetheless stood his ground, masking his fear. If John were to kill him now, he would not show him weakness. As John grew closer he raised his dagger high above his head.

Everything seemed to slow down and unfold right before their eyes. The guards fighting in the background and their swords clanged against each other to defend their kings. Wendy stared up at her brother with betrayal seeing as he meant to kill her love.

John knocked over plates and cups in his path and Noah pulled Mary back from the scene, scared that he might turn the other way and try to attack them.

John stopped at the end of the table and brought his dagger down to pierce Gregory's heart. Just before the tip of the blade touched his shirt, Wendy shoved him out of the way, taking the hit instead. Her face contorted in pain as the dagger entered her chest and pierced her heart, killing her in an instant.

Gregory fell to the floor catching his dead wife who lay limply in his arms. He gasped in heartbreak as blood gushed out from Wendy's chest, coating her white dress with the red sticky substance. Gregory looked up, meeting John's eyes that held no remorse.

"GUARDS! KILL HIM!" he roared.

He watched as John fled with Alexander and his two guards who had managed to slice the Tay soldiers' necks open. John and Alexander fought their way out the doors of Tay with the two guards by their sides. They hopped onto their horses' backs, taking off through the large gates just before they closed. They rode fast as arrows shot at them hitting one of John's men. The man howled in pain as he fell off his horse to the ground with an arrow sticking out of his arm.

"Wait! Don't leave me!" he yelled out, hoping they would turn back around.

But they didn't.

The man turned around seeing the Tay soldiers running towards him. He panicked not wanting to be tortured and put in the dungeons. Cowardly he unsheathed his dagger from his side and held it against his own neck, slicing it open. The Tay soldiers stopped before him as his lifeless body fell to the ground with blood gushing out from his neck.

Back in the dining room, Noah clasped his hand over his mouth in shock.

Tears slid rapidly down his pure face.

"Mom?" he whimpered.

He hoped that maybe she would answer back, saying she was fine.

But she didn't.

All that was heard were the king's sobs. Gregory gathered himself together and spoke with a few stutters.

"Noah…M-Mary. Go to y-you're ro-oms…you do not want to see this."

The two obeyed and left out into the hallway that was filled with an eerie silence.

Noah suddenly broke down, sobs wracked his body. Mary could feel his pain.

Gently she reached out to place a comforting hand on his shoulder, but before she could touch him, he took off down the hallway. Noah took long strides and made it to his room within a matter of seconds. With a shaky hand he reached out to open the door but could not seem to find his grip. He leaned his head against the door suppressing a sob. Mary slowly walked to his side wearing a remorseful expression and opened the door for him and closed it behind for privacy.

Noah let a loud sob escape from his mouth that could be heard faintly through the castle. It broke Mary's heart. His chest heaved up and down uncontrollable as he slumped down onto his bed burying his face into his pillow.

"Oh gosh. No! No…please no."

***

The sounds of horses galloping in the night could be heard nearing the iron gates of Caesar's castle. The guards in watchtowers high above stood on alert and aimed their crossbows at the three hooded figures.

"State your name and business here in Caesars kingdom!" the head guard shouted.

"I am your king you fool!" John shouted back, pulling his hood down to reveal his face. The guard's eyes widened.

"I-I am sorry…Your Majesty."

"Just open the damn gate!"

The guard obeyed, pulling a lever. The wooden gates slowly opened with a creak and John quickly rode in jumping flat on the ground.

Alexander rode up next to him and stepped to the ground wearing a look of guilt. A large red flag high above the castle blew in the wind showing the symbol of a blade pierced through a heart. John and his son walked up a row of marble steps to the grand wooden doors of the castle. Just before John could open them himself, they swung open to reveal his advisor. Micheal came running out and stopped them.

"My lords…what are you doing back so early?"

"Our trip had to be cut short," John replied coldly.

"Why? What happened over there?" Micheal asked, already assuming the worst had happened.

John ignored him and walked past the confused man with a blank expression. Alexander went to follow him through the doors before being stopped once more by Micheal grabbing ahold of his shoulder.

"Don't touch me!" he sneered, pushing the hand away.

"Sorry, Your Highness but please…tell me what happened in Tay," Micheal implored.

The young prince sighed. "My father killed the queen."

His face then turned cold like his father's as he disappeared into the castle.

Michael's eyes widened as soon as he took in those words. Wendy could not have been dead…could she? Quickly he ran in after the king, following him into the throne room and jumped in front of John.

"You killed your sister!"

"Do not raise your voice to me!" John yelled in a powerful voice and pushed past Micheal, plopping down in his cushioned throne chair.

"King Gregory Tay has one of the most powerful armies in Lotogettar."

"So," John replied carelessly

"You killed his queen." Micheal felt his heart break as he let those words fall from his tongue but continued locking away his feelings. "The king of Tay will not take this lightly. This is the start of a new war."

John looked directly into his eyes. "Then I shall fight."

Micheal nodded, knowing he could not reason with him and began to leave.

"There is something else."

Micheal stopped and turned back to face him. "What is it?"

"It could be nothing, but could you get me that book that tells of Tay's history? That's an order!"

Chapter Eight

Two days had passed since Wendy's death and all of Tay had been quiet. The people from town were notified about the queen's death and were all waiting to be let through the gates for their loveable queen's funeral.

Mary woke up that depressing morning, walking out onto her balcony. A gust of wind blew past her, making her shiver. It was colder than usual.

"*Falye hiskon.* (fall season) That is why you're cold," Noah explained from his balcony.

Mary spun her head towards him. She hadn't seen the prince since Wendy's death. He was seated in a chair covered with a blanket and his blond hair blew with the wind.

Noah turned to Mary, giving her a small smile despite his tearstained face. Looking closer she saw dark bags under his eyes.

"Were you out here all night?" she asked.

Yawning tiredly he replied, "Um…yeah. I could not fall asleep."

She frowned at his words, feeling even more bad for him. "You should get some sleep."

He gave her a sad smile. "I cannot right now. It is almost time for my mother's funeral. You will be there with me…right?"

"I'll be right by your side."

And she did stand by his side along with Jenna.

The poor woman would not stop crying. The people of Tay all dressed in black wore solemn looks and some shed tears. Everyone stood out in the silent gardens. Only a few whispers were heard here and there. Women, men, and children walked past, saying a quick prayer for their queen who lay peacefully still in her casket.

As soon as they were done sending their condolences, Gregory moved from the side to in front of his deceased wife and began to speak as tears gathered in his eyes.

"Keensa Wendy vil a jera, Analay…irosa lunda bi anot. Ban har Keensa vil mayan rim gal…Kinsa John Caesar talted regis lesta har Keensa!" (Queen Wendy was a ruler, mother…wife, loved by all. But our queen was taken from us. King John Caesar committed regicide against our queen!)

The crowd erupted in gasps and loud whispering that soon turned into loud bickering. Some cursed Caesar's name.

"Lye Kinsa! Shil dal fote plargro?" (My King! Will we go to war?) one person yelled from the crowd.

Gregory sighed and turned to his advisor, Kennings. *"Cado favi jeds fale tanoen cual te jalga."* (Please have guards escort everyone back to town.)

Kennings nodded, gathering a couple guards up and ordering them to bring the people safely back to town. The guards began pushing the crowd out. They were having a tough time doing so, though, since some were too stubborn to leave without a straight answer from their king.

Sooner or later the gardens were cleared out.

Jenna walked off as if it was too much to bear seeing Wendy, her good friend, lying there limply. The two watched as Gregory kneeled down before his wife. He shakingly grabbed Wendy's hands that were folded neatly across her stomach holding a bouquet of white roses. Her favorite flowers. Mumbling a quick prayer under his breath, he kissed her cold forehead, staying there for a whole minute. A tear fell from his eye onto Wendy's closed one, rolling down the side of her cheek.

Noah walked over and placed a hand on his father's shoulder. "What do we do from here on?"

Gregory wiped his tears away and stood up, putting on a brave face for his son. "Today we mourn…tomorrow we prepare for battle."

Turning back around he took the blue velvet blanket that was folded up at the end of Wendy's casket and gently draped it over her.

"We shall meet again soon, my love," he whispered and walked back into his home.

Together Noah and Mary stepped forward and said a quick prayer before they left to walk through the quiet gardens. No birds were chirping, or horses neighing. It seemed the whole world grew quiet for the queen.

As they wandered onto a stone pathway, Noah held a protective arm around Mary's shoulders. Suddenly Noah stopped, planting himself in front of Mary. He looked down, placing his hands on her shoulders.

"Mary, you must promise me something."

She frowned watching as a tear fell from his eye.

"Of course. We're friends…friends keep promises."

Though he didn't show it, her comment made him more upset.

"Dark times are to arrive. Promise you will be safe and not leave me."

Mary pulled him into a tight hug.

"I will never leave you…I promise."

Wrapping his arms around her waist Noah buried his head into the crook of her neck.

For the first time he realized he truly loved her.

Chapter Nine

A busy day was to come. Noah stood with his father, attending his first royal council meeting. High nobles from the Fenter Kingdom were called to attend the meeting to help fight the Caesars. They were currently arguing about what to do for battle.

"We should go over there and surprise attack them!" one yelled.

"We should not attack first! We should wait," another suggested from across the room.

All of this was boring to Noah. Gregory had woken him up early that morning to inform him of a council meeting taking place and said Noah was to accompany him to the meeting. Noah was thrilled about going to his first meeting wearing a jubilant smile as he entered the room full of nobles. But as his headache worsened, the young prince regretted tagging along.

"Enough of this petty arguing! As we bicker, not even figuring out a plan, King John could already be marching his soldiers over here right now ready to attack at any given second," Gregory yelled over them.

"My father is right. We should not wait. It will only slow us down. We need to act quickly before something happens," Noah declared, speaking up for the first time since he got there.

"And what do you know of war…*boy*."

Noah peered up to see a man by the name of Brandon Sealies. He was an older strong warrior who was the Fenter Kingdom's most trusted advisor.

"Enough to know that you have to be ready for the worst and not stand by when you know you could be doing something."

The man stayed quiet.

"My son is right."

"Well, I am sorry, but we do not want to ruin our alliance with the Caesars. So it looks like you will be fighting this war on your own."

Gregory was beyond mad at Brandon's words and ended the meeting right then and there. Everyone left the room in a dour mood, sending scowls towards each other.

Gregory was left alone with his son, pinching the bridge of his nose. Something he did a lot to contain his anger. "Noah, I have something important to ask you." Gregory turned to his son looking serious. "Do you—"

"Your majesty!" A frantic-looking guard came in. "There was an incident in the town. The people are in a panic and we cannot seem to calm them down!"

Gregory sighed, growing more aggravated than he already was. "What could possibly be the problem?"

"You have to see for yourself…it's bad." The guard hurried off.

"Come along, son. We must contain the situation."

"But what about how I am not allowed back there," Noah asked, following after his father.

"I will make an exception for today."

As they hurried out and neared the town entrance, sounds of panic and cries for help were heard. The king and his son shared a concerned glance and sped up their pace as more guards followed behind. In a matter of seconds, they arrived at the horrendous scene. Nine citizens lay dead in the town of Tay.

Three women, four men, and two children were spread out within a couple of feet of each other with an arrow through their heads. The families of the victims held them in their arms not caring of the blood dripping on them.

Other's ran away in horror, scared that they would be next. Noah gasped not knowing what to think of the situation as Gregory grew even more infuriated.

He yelled out to his guards as he walked over to an old man who lay dead, leaning upright on a stone building.

"*Seek roe aki shyds laya diy esa seas finlash seisa!*" (Search for the spies who did this and kill them!)

Gripping the iron made arrow he ripped it out of the wide-eyed man's head.

A folded piece of paper with specks of dark blood dripping from it, hung from the middle. Snagging the paper off, Gregory opened it up and began to read aloud for all to hear.

"I, John Caesar of Caesar's kensattar…feer bi fenfare plargro ono Tay kensattar. Ini tren vens alatiyraiis…midway between our kingdoms." (I, John Caesar of Caesar's Kingdom… here by declaring war upon the Kingdom of Tay…in two days we meet at sunrise).

The few people that stayed listened closely.

"I want everyone to take shelter in their homes and not leave!"

Gregory commanded all the people. He cared for his people greatly, which was one thing Noah looked up to. He wanted to be like him one day.

Rain began to fall from the cloudy sky above. Everyone ran to their homes, looking for security. The bereaved ones stayed behind covering the dead with blankets.

"My king!" a guard came running back with others, panting heavily.

"We searched everywhere but could not find anyone."

"Gather up all the guards…choose some to stay back. Tomorrow we leave for battle at first light."

***

Mary let out an anxious sigh. She sat on the cold floor right before the balcony opened up. Holding her knees to her chest, she listened carefully as raindrops fell softly from the night sky above and the silk curtains moved smoothly with the wind.

Earlier on she heard the faint noise of cries of panic. She hadn't seen Noah all day and worried, thinking something bad happened. Maybe that he was down below crying out for help. Thinking over everything from the past few days, Mary sighed with stress.

She wondered if her mother was worried.

The poor woman was probably searching everywhere for her child and Max, he was probably lonely without her.

The only thing keeping Mary from being homesick was Noah. The two had a connection. They acted as if they knew each other for so long and even though Mary only met Noah days ago, she had developed a fondness for the handsome blond.

Though they could never be together. Lotogettar was his world; Mary was from another. The thought made Mary depressed. What happens when she goes home? If she goes home. She may never see Noah again.

Knock! Knock!

"Come in," Mary said softly.

The door slowly creaked open and footsteps were heard approaching her small figure. Noah's tall figure sat down closely next to her, leaving just a tiny gap between them.

"What happened down there? I heard yelling," Mary whispered, looking up at Noah.

The crystal walls surrounding them illuminated off his fair skin, making his blond hair glow like gold.

"Nothing you need to worry about."

He wore a slight distressed look. Seeing this, Mary decided to not question him further and gently rested her head on his shoulder. He leaned his head against hers. They sat there in silence listening to the soft rain, but the peace could not stay as Mary could still feel Noah's tense state.

"What's wrong? You know you can tell me anything."

Lifting his head off hers, he looked down and faced her with a serious expression.

"Tomorrow we go to war."

War.

That word left a sour taste on Mary's tongue as it left his mouth. The last time someone she loved went to war, they never came back. Tilting her head to face his, she began to worry.

"Are you going to be fighting?"

Though Mary feared she already knew the answer to her question. He gave her a short nod. A tear sprang free from her eye at that.

"Why do you cry…*lye lunda?*" Noah grabbed her face gently in his hands, wiping the tear away with his thumb.

"I-I don't want to lose you." A small crack sounded in her voice.

"Do not worry. You will never lose me and I am a great fighter. After all. I was trained to be the best," he boasted, lifting up her hopes.

***

The rain continued on into the next day, pouring harder than before. The strong wind blew large drops of water into Noah and Mary's faces. They stood out by the front gates watching as an army of two thousand soldiers marched out through the gates, stopping in the field out front, awaiting for their king's next orders.

The soldiers wore leather tunics with matching pants and long-laced boots. Over their chests was a silver chainmail with matching helmets. At their sides were silver swords with a crystal hilt.

Mary turned to stare at Noah's winsome, hard, glaring face. His hair had turned a darker shade just like Mary's red hair had from being soaked with water. Glancing back at her, he put on an endearing grin. Noah gently pushed a wet strand of hair out of her face.

"You look funny when your hair is wet." He laughed a bit, but in a quick second his expression turned serious. "Mary, I will be gone for a couple of days. Whatever you do, promise me you will not leave the castle."

"I'll promise if you promise to come back," Mary replied sternly.

Noah sighed. "Remember what I told you last night? I will never leave you."

Just as he finished speaking, Gregory, on horseback, rode out of the gates, slowly walking down a row of soldiers as rain pelted his face. Riding back over to his son, he tapped his shoulder visibly annoyed. "You're lucky we had an extra one." Gregory threw a helmet into his son's gloved hands.

"Thank you, Father."

Before putting on the helmet, Noah turned to Mary, pulling her into a tight hold.

"Farewell, Mary… *sholundalia.* Till we meet again," he whispered in the shell of her ear and kissed her forehead gently.

Turning back around without looking back, Noah hopped onto his horse galloping over to his father's side. Orders and commands were shouted through the air.

"We will not allow the miserable King of Caesar to continue his cruel acts! The queen shall be avenged and we will defeat that monster!" Gregory yelled, hyping up his men.

They all yelled back, cheering him on and all took off, ready to chop off the head of John Caesar.

Mary watched the large group grow smaller as they rode farther away. An uncanny feeling overcame her. Her stomach began to knot and a sudden ache moved throughout her head.

"Lady Mary! Let's get you inside before you get sick," Jenna exclaimed, pulling her back to the castle.

Before Mary could even take a step in, her vision clouded over. Jenna began speaking once more, but it sounded like her head was under water. And before she knew it, she was plummeting to the ground.

Soldiers were lined up on either side of Mary and charged towards each other. The ground rumbled beneath her, but the world around her was quiet.

Mary ducked down in fear covering her face as they grew closer. She squeezed her eyes awaiting the impact. But it never came. Uncovering her eyes, Mary looked around to see they went right through her as if she were a ghost.

The soldiers slowly turned into a dark shadowy mist swirling around Mary while she crawled on her hands and knees searching for a way out. She stumbled out from the dark clouds and into the light. The shadows suddenly turned back into the soldiers who swung their swords viciously at each other, and there he was. Noah came speeding through riding on top of his horse. Charging towards the enemy. Noah swung his sword down, swiftly cutting a man's head off. Blood splattered on his face and in his blond hair.

Mary continued to watch as an older man ran into the picture. He was stronger than Noah and ran past, slashing at the horse's legs. The horse neighed in pain and stood up on its hind legs throwing Noah off its back to the ground. Noah quickly jumped back up onto his feet sneering at the man. The older man swung his sword furiously at the young prince, being blocked each time. Noah then briskly pressed his foot to the man's chest, pushing him to the ground. Walking closer he pointed this sword at the man's neck to finish him off. Mary kept her eyes directly on Noah. She could not hold it in anymore.

"Noah!"

Noah froze.

His eyes widened, turning his head in Mary's direction. Locking eyes with her he mumbled something under his breath and stepped forward but froze in place once more.

Noah's face twisted in pain. The sick sound of someone being impaled and their bones cracking fell upon Mary's ears. Turning to glance behind, Noah saw the man back on his feet wearing a malevolent smirk. He peered down to see the metal sword sticking out through his chest. Dark red blood dripping off the blade.

The man pulled it out laughing madly and running off to slay another.

"NO!" Mary screamed in agony, watching as Noah fell to the ground with a thump. She didn't hesitate to run over to his side cradling his head in her lap. Coughing up blood, he used all his strength to place a hand on her cheek. Mary held it there as he spoke groggily.

"Your dress...it will get dirty."

The blue velvet dress she wore soaked up with blood, but she did not care about one measly dress.

"You're dying. I don't care about one dress."

"It was my mothersss...," he slurred a bit as he spoke.

"Your life is worth more than some dress. You can't leave me...you promised," she cried softly, pushing a lock of sweaty hair out of his face.

"Mary...not all promises are meant to be kept," he said sadly, coughing up more blood.

"But you need to do something for me."

"Anything," she whispered as her tears fell on his cold skin. She would do anything for the boy. Even if it meant dying with him.

"Wake up."

Chapter Ten

Gasping for air, Mary jolted up from a bed with tear-filled eyes. She sniffled a bit, feeling her wet teary face and let a sob fall past her lips.

"Oh gosh. Please no…."

Mary clasped a hand over her mouth. Pushing the silk blankets off of her sweaty body… She curled into a small ball and let the tears spring freely from her eyes.

The door opened, but she paid no mind to whomever it was, not caring if they saw her breaking down.

"Mary, you're awake! I just stepped out for a bit and—" Jenna stopped herself from speaking as her smile faded upon seeing Mary's body wracked with sobs. "Oh you poor girl. Whatever is the matter?" She immediately went to the weeping girl's side.

"N-noah…he's gone. He…," Mary sobbed, not even being able to finish.

"Do not worry. He is alright. It was just a dream."

Jenna rubbed her back in a motherly way. Grabbing a handkerchief from the bedside table, she pushed away Mary's hair from her face and wiped away her tears.

"Where am I?" Mary asked, gathering herself up and peering around the small room.

"You're in the healing room. You passed out only seconds after the army left for war. You were asleep for two whole days…I was starting to worry."

"Two days…are they back? Is Noah here?" She finally met Jenna's eyes.

"No…they have only just arrived to battle."

***

Gregory and Noah rode with pride on top of their horses, holding their heads high. Behind them Gregory's army marched loudly through the grassy field, holding flags of Tay Kingdom on poles high above. Soon they came to a halt waiting for the sun to rise. It was silent until Gregory turned to his son, speaking firmly.

"Son…if anything is to happen to me I want you to go back to the castle."

Noah scoffed, laughing a little. He was a little too prideful. "Father, if anything is to happen, I am going to stay by your side."

"Your mother, brother and I have decided long ago that you were to be the heir to the throne of Tay. You will be rid of your stubbornness and listen to me when I say so. End of story," Gregory shot back as his son, who let out a frustrated huff. He knew he would not win a conversation battle over his father, but yet he still tried.

The orange and blue hues began to rise over the horizon of thick trees and hills farther off to the side. Noah grew nervous thinking the Caesar army would charge at them any second.

"Son…if you're scared you do not have to fight. This is your first battle after all."

"I am not scared! Besides…there is always a first for everything," Noah replied angrily, glaring at the few guards who laughed at him. "I want to fight."

A smile graced the king's lips at Noah's courage. He reminded him of when he was younger, going into his first battle.

Gregory's smile soon vanished at the sound of marching and the all-too familiar sound of swords clanging against each other. He put on his fierce, intimidating look that scared all lords in Lotogettar as he watched King John Caesar in the distance sitting on top of his horse with Alexander riding next to him. They both wore the same leather clothes along with chainmail and matching swords. Parading behind was an army of one thousand men.

"My brother!" John said with sarcasm as he put a hand up to signal the soldiers to stop.

"Do not call me that!"

"Oh…why not? You were married to my sister…after all," John slurred, sounding like he drank a few too much.

"Morning has just begun and you're already drunk?" Gregory laughed mockingly.

John scoffed and continued on with a dramatic drunken sigh, "Why do we fight?"

Gregory stared blankly at the drunk fool. "You killed my wife."

John looked like a mad man with his red puffy eyes and mouth agape as he listened closely to Gregory's every word. The deranged man then burst out with laughter, being the only one until his son joined in.

"Shut up, boy!" John scolded his son and slapped him in the back of the head harshly. Alexander shut up quickly and winced a bit, rubbing his head in pain.

Noah frowned, almost feeling bad for his cousin.

"Yes, I did do that, but there's something else we fight for. Or someone…is there not?" He raised a drunken brow at Gregory before continuing. "That red-haired girl you hide within your walls…she is a part of something big, isn't she? You could hand her over to me if you want to avoid war. She could be a slave here. Be drowned with riches… I could make her a queen or she could be my whor—"

"SHUT UP! You leave her out of this," Noah shouted protectively.

John laughed at his nephew. "You don't like that plan? Fine, we can go with the other one. All of us together as a family can march back over to Tay Kingdom and rip her from those wretched walls and hang her from the highest tower for the whole world of Lotogettar to see!"

It wasn't just Noah who grew more irate at his words. It was also Alexander. He glared at his father with hatred. The thought of the girl who they had both come to love dying in such a horrific way…it made them want to chop off the head of anyone who tried to hurt Mary.

"I see you're not fond of those ideas…so shall we begin this fight?" John questioned with a drunken smirk.

Gregory raised his sword to the sky angrily. If anyone touched Mary the wrong way, he would kill them. He knew his son cared deeply for the girl and would not allow him to be grief-stricken like he was.

"Kill that deranged king along with anyone who gets in your way! CHARGE!" Gregory shouted to his soldiers.

The strong warriors behind him let out battle cries and charged at the enemy. Some ran and some sped past them on horses as John's soldiers reduplicated their actions. Noah stayed back with his father for a few seconds before riding full speed into battle. They clashed together in one big cluster, spilling blood at each swing of their swords. The Tay army had the advantage of having more soldiers and horses then the Caesar army. Noah and Gregory rode side by side cutting men's heads off with a single swing of their sword.

Throughout the battle, Noah and his father split up losing sight of each other. As Noah rode through the field still on his horse, Alexander rode fast on his horse past him. He whipped his arm at Noah's chest knocking the wind out of him as he fell to the ground dropping his sword.

Noah stood swiftly back up to his feet as his helmet rolled off his head and watched his horse run away in fear. Looking back to his cousin, Noah masked his fear. Alexander dropped his sword and walked closer, punching him in the face.

"We're even now," Alexander sneered gripping his shoulders and pulling him closer. "Once we win this battle, Mary is gonna be mine."

Noah glanced behind his cousin's head to see his father and his uncle fighting. John took one swift swing and stumbled to the ground as Gregory moved out of the way, not even having to defend himself. Noah watched as John's own metal blade pierced right through his neck. His head hung loosely off his shoulders as blood poured out. Noah turned back to his cousin and smirked.

"You've already lost! I can read right through your patheticness…Mary will never love yo—"

Clonk!

***

It had been almost four days since Mary woke up. Ever since then, she would sit down by the gates waiting till sunset, searching for any sign of Noah's return. Mary shivered a bit as a cold gust of wind blew past. She sat by the gates, staring out into the thick fog.

"Lady Mary," a deep rich voice spoke up.

Her warm cloak was placed gently on her shoulders. She glided a hand over the green velvet material and looked up to the boy.

"Thank you for finding it for me, Maxwell."

"You're welcome. But do not mind if I ask…you have been staying out here till the sunsets every day since you have woken up…why?" the young guard asked.

He had met Mary only a couple days ago and would accompany her while she sat here waiting. Mary connected easily with the boy. He reminded her a lot like Max back home. In fact he looked strangely similar to him. The only difference was his brown hair was longer.

"I'm just worried that's all."

"Well, you should be…you are *prydalia* after all."

"What does that mean?" Mary questioned, sending him an odd look.

"Did you not hear what the prince said? Oh right…you do not speak our language. *Prydalia* means *the prince's lover*." He spoke as if it were obvious.

A red hue washed over Mary's cheeks.

"But he never said that word to me before."

"Not that one…the word he spoke to you before leaving for battle."

A grin fell on his face as Mary thought for a second, then remembered. She was meaning to ask Noah what it meant once he returned but forgot all about it.

"Do you mean *sholu*—"

"*Sholundalia.* It means *I love you*," he interrupted.

Mary blushed even more.

"You mean that he—"

Maxwell cut her off once more.

"Yes, my friend…the Prince of Tay loves you."

A bright smile appeared on her face as shock and joy filled her.

"Do you love him?" he asked.

"Yes I do. But why me? I'm nothing special."

He placed a gentle hand on her shoulder wearing a sad smile.

"Mary…you are a fair lady. Any man would be out of his mind if—"

He stopped short as the sound of horses galloping neared the castle. Maxwell immediately changed his stance and stood on alert. His once kindhearted self turned into a belligerent soldier. Maxwell unsheathed his sword, standing in front of Mary, ready to defend and give his life for hers.

Appearing out from the thick fog was a horse rider holding on to a limp body in their arms. The rider drew closer and stopped before the two. He took off his helmet to reveal himself as the king. Maxwell immediately dropped his weapon and fell into a bow.

"Your Majesty. Forgive me for raising a weapon at you."

"It is alright, Maxwell. You show great loyalty to my kingdom."

Mary poked her head out from behind Maxwell's tall figure and walked towards Gregory. She eyed the person in his arms and gasped. She could recognize Noah's blond hair with specks of blood that ran through the golden locks. Mary tried getting a closer look before Gregory pulled his horse away.

"Mary wait-—"

"Is he alright?"

"Yes, he has just been knocked out, that's all."

"Can I see him?"

"Yes…but first let's bring him to the healing room."

Gregory turned to Maxwell. "The army should be back soon, but we lost two hundred and fifty were injured. Prepare to help."

***

"You love him, don't you?" Gregory spoke in a mere whisper.

Mary nodded with a soft smile and stared at Noah who was laid down in the same bed Mary woke up in. He had a bloody gash on his forehead that was not too deep. A nurse took off his sweaty, bloody shirt to check for other wounds. Only a few scratches were seen. His chest barely rose with a breath. The nurse soon finished mending his wounds, finishing it off with a bandage wrapped around his head.

"Whatever happens, Mary...be there for my son, please. Do not let his stubbornness get the best of him," Gregory said before acknowledging the nurse who walked over to the two.

"I finished fixing his wounds. He should be fine and wake up soon. But do not let him move around too much for a couple of days. I'll leave you with him," she said, leaving them alone.

"I have to go. When he wakes up...call for me," Gregory said, following the nurse out and closing the door behind.

Mary sighed sadly and pulled over a small wooden chair next to the bed. She grabbed Noah's hand that hung limply off the side gently gliding her thumb over the top. Peering down at him, she watched as his chest with minor scars rose slowly up and down. Silently she prayed he would wake up soon, staring at his pale face, patiently waiting for his bright blue eyes to open.

Chapter Eleven

Time seemed to go by slowly as Mary sat by Noah's side for a while now. The wooden chair was becoming more and more uncomfortable as her patience slowly broke away. Looking away from Noah, tears welled up in her green eyes.

"Come on. Please wake up…I love you," she mumbled, squeezing his hand gently. Still he would not make a sound. Only thing was his chest rising up and down slowly.

She was starting to lose hope and then…he weakly squeezed her hand back. Mary smiled brightly as he began to stir.

"Mary…is that you?"

"Yes, it's me."

A small smile appeared on his face. He finally opened his eyes, staring back at her. Wincing a bit at the brightness around, he held his head, feeling a migraine coming on.

"What happened?"

"You tell me."

Noah groaned and went to sit up. He struggled stubbornly as Mary held him down. Squinting his eyes he winced each time as his head ached with pain.

"Last thing I remember is my uncle holding his sword the wrong way and falling on it…cutting open his neck…and my cousin. He could have killed me, but he didn't."

He used all his strength to lean on his elbows.

"No. You have to rest…lay back down," Mary said, keeping her hand on his cold chest and gently trying to push him back down. He grabbed her hand, stopping her.

"I am fine…I have rested enough."

Noah sat farther up, pushing the covers off and planting his feet on the cold ground. They sat in silence staring at each other awkwardly thinking of what to say next.

"*Sholundalia,*" Mary said in a low whisper.

Noah's expression was unreadable. He did not know if he heard her correctly and asked, "What did you say?"

"*Sholundalia…*Noah," she repeated louder, wearing a bright smile. Mirroring her smile Noah placed his hand on the back of Mary's neck, pulling her closer and pressed their foreheads together. Gently he placed his soft lips on hers.

Kissing him back slowly, Mary placed a hand on the side of his face, moving next to him on the bed and deepened the kiss. He pulled away, leaving barely any space between each other.

"Ever since I met you in those woods, I felt a feeling I have never felt before. The next day I asked my mother…she told me it was love." He stared into her eyes lovingly.

Mary caressed the side of his face, gently gliding her thumb over his bottom lip.

"Then that means I feel the exact same way."

Noah wrapped his arms tighter around her waist and pulled her down next to him. Mary rested her head on his chest and yawned.

"Go to sleep, *lye lunda.*" Noah softly ran his fingers through her soft hair.

"I still do not know what that means," Mary mumbled tiredly.

Noah began to doze off and mumbled, "It means, my love."

A faint smile appeared on her face as she dozed off as well into a deep slumber….

***

"*Wake up my love.*"

A smile fell over Mary's lips as she felt a pair of lips kiss her cheek. Opening her eyes she watched as Noah walked across the room, grabbing a white loose tunic hanging over a chair. He placed it over his shoulders and buttoned it up. Mary stretched her arms and yawned, standing up.

"You know…you're really not supposed to walk around," Mary said. Noah walked over to her and leaned down pressing a quick kiss to her lips.

"I have no serious injuries. I'll be fine," he insisted. His hands lifted to his head where the white bandage was wrapped tightly around his forehead and began to unravel it.

"Stop that." Mary grabbed his hands, re-wrapping the bandage. "You have a bad head injury."

"Yeah and it just got worse," Noah whined as she wrapped the bandage even more tighter than before.

"It's for your health. But since you insist you're fine and definitely won't go back to bed…I want you to meet someone. Come on," Mary said with a smile and grabbed his hand, pulling him through the halls. They wandered the halls until Mary came to a halt as she spotted Maxwell across the hall.

"Maxwell!" Mary waved him down. He came running and pulled Mary into a hug. Noah stood to the side and watched with jealousy.

"Ahem."

Maxwell let Mary go and turned to Noah, bowing.

"Your Highness. It is an honor to speak to you."

Noah's face softened and the jealousy went away. Someone actually wanted to speak to him.

"You do not need to bow to me…friend."

***

Weeks passed since everything, and it was calm, a bit too calm, though. The village was quiet. Gregory held a feast for everyone to mourn the loss of loved ones, but nobody came, still too afraid to leave their homes. Gregory assured the people everything was back in order but they would not budge.

"The people are still too afraid to leave their homes." Noah told Mary as he held her in his arms peering over the balcony, looking down at the town.

"Well, maybe we can go down there and convince them somehow," Mary suggested. Noah chuckled a bit.

"The people of Tay are very stubborn…if they didn't listen to my father, they definitely won't listen to me…and I don't think most of the people are too fond of you, besides everyone who lives in this castle. They will not even give you a second glance."

Mary frowned at his words. "Why not…why don't they like me? Did I do something wrong?"

She turned to face him. A cold breeze blew harshly past the two, making them even more cold than they already were.

"You did nothing wrong…they are just jealous. Anyways it is very cold…we should move back into the warmth. We could catch some sort of illness. People die every year from the *Foldrain flu*," he complained.

Mary laughed squirming out of his arms.

"What's the *Foldrain flu?*"

"It's a dreadful sickness where your insides fold and squish together, causing hallucinations and then—WAIT! Don't do that!" Noah suddenly yelled out, watching as Mary climbed up barefoot onto the railing. It was just as wide as her feet.

"I thought you were scared of heights," he said, nervously watching her put one foot in front of the other.

"That was different…I was hanging off the side of a building. Here I'm not…I'm simply walking along in a line where if I do fall there are two options…one of those is that I can actually survive."

Noah scoffed. "This is completely reckless! One wrong move and you can fall. What do I have to do to keep you out of harm's way…move you into my chambers?"

Mary raised a brow, glancing at him. "You don't always have to protect me…besides I am always careful. See?"

She stretched her arms out as if she was ready to fly and swiftly spun back around taking slow steps the other way.

"Mary, please come down from there…I do not want to watch the one I love fall to her death!"

"You don't need to worry…as I said before—"

RAWRRRR!

A loud inhuman sound rumbled through the kingdom, causing all buildings to shake violently.

"Whoa!"

Mary suddenly lost her balance and stumbled backwards. She let out a loud scream squeezing her eyes shut awaiting to hit the long drop down below. But in a fast motion Noah jumped forward, tightly capturing her in his arms. Noah pulled her away from the railing and held her close in his arms. Both were on the verge of tears. Their hearts beat hard with fear. Noah placed his forehead on hers as his voice trembled.

"A-are you okay? Don't ever do that again! I-I thought I lost you for good." His chest heaved up and down as he scolded her.

"I'm sorry…you won't lose me. Ever." Mary shook with fear.

The two walked back into Mary's warm room, still holding each other in fear.

"What was that?"

"That was the second part of the prophecy."

He pulled her along out into the hallway.

"What's this prophecy?"

Noah stopped and turned to her. "All I can tell you is that you're a part of it."

"Why can't you tell me anything else?"

Noah caressed the side of her face, pushing a strand of red hair behind her ear. "I just want you to be safe. Okay?" Mary nodded and he pulled her hand running down the hall. Suddenly Maxwell appeared frantically in front of them.

"My friends! I was looking everywhere for you two," he exclaimed, panting heavily, out of breath as if he had just ran from one kingdom to another.

"Maxwell. What's the matter?" Noah looked to his friend. Over the days they had gotten to know each other and for Mary's sake became friends.

"The king wishes to see you both at the front gates."

***

"Father, you called for us?" Noah asked, standing next to his father who stood by the gates staring out at nothing.

"Oh…there you two are. Thank goodness you're both alright." Gregory looked relieved. Breaking from his gaze he turned to the young couple.

"What is a Caesar flag doing here?" Noah asked, motioning towards the red flag in his hands.

"Your cousin…now the King of Caesar has brought his army over here ready to attack. They fled like cowards when that wretched beast cried out."

He wore a cold glare.

Wosh! Crackle!

The three jerked their heads to the side at the sudden loud sound of wind burning against the wind. Gregory took long strides to stand between the quiet village and the large castle. Noah and Mary ran after him, stopping in their tracks behind him and gaping at the sight before them. Guards began lining up behind them as they stared up at the mountains.

A long line of fiery red flames blew out from a cave on the side of the mountains. Mary gasped as others stared in awe. The people in town finally opened their doors to see the commotion. Panic filled their faces as they looked on.

"It's the dragon!"

"The prophecy is true to its words!"

People yelled running around frantically. Vicious bangs came from the mountain as the beast tried breaking through the metal bars that held it in.

Gregory took out his sword and his guards followed pointing their bows up towards the giant hills. Some guards were shaking with fear, having second thoughts about coming to stand behind there king and kill the beast

Bang! Bang! BANG! Crash!?

The large heavy doors that once held the beast in came flying to the ground. Noah protectively pushed Mary behind him and unsheathed his sword masking his scared expression with a brave one. The world grew eerily quiet. Black smoke blew out from the cave.

"What's he waiting for?" Noah asked.

His father grew angrier with each given second staring up at the mountains.

"I don't know. But he has been in there for far too long. SHOW YOURSELF, YOU COWARD!?"

BOOM!

There, a dragon greater and larger than any other, broke out from the cave. Large rocks slammed to the ground. The beast stretched its large scaly green wings to flap about. Its claws grew long and sharp. Everyone stepped back in fear except for the king. Gregory staired the beast directly in its malevolent yellow, piercing eyes. The beast reared its large green head back and let out a deafening roar. The dragon soared down towards them opening its mouth wide and showing off the sharp yellow teeth within.

Noah's eyes widened and he pulled Mary in his arms to the ground as his father and the nearby guards ducked down as it swooshed past them. Just as its long scaly tail whipped passed them, Noah sprung back up and sliced off the end of it.

The dragon screeched in pain as a large chunk of the tail fell to the ground. Small drops of black blood splattered along Noah and Mary's faces. The dragon drove high into the sky, whipping around and staring down at the town and fleeing people. He spit his noxious flames at them. People fled as lines of fire tunneled through town. Houses burned to ashes quickly. The few people who hadn't found an exit were now surrounded by the flames, screaming in pain as it spread along their bodies.

"Noah, take Mary and go inside the castle. Do not leave until this is over," Gregory yelled over the chaos.

"I will take Mary to safety, but I will come back to help you fight this monster!"

"You will go and stay there! You will not survive this battle. These people will need you. The Kingdom of Tay will need you…and Mary needs you." Gregory pulled his son in for one last hug.

"I love you, Father. I hope to see you after battle." Noah teared up a bit. He had a feeling this would be the last time they spoke.

"I'm proud of you, son…. Now go."

Gregory practically shoved him and Mary back to the castle. Noah tugged Mary along, pulling her back to the castle's gates. Mary's mouth agape, she finally tore her eyes from the monstrous creature. Stopping before they entered the castle, Noah took her face in his hands checking for injuries.

"Are you okay?"

"I—" Mary stopped short her breath hitching in her throat. A dark shadow flew over them.

"Come on!"

The two ran towards the castle doors as the dragon blew flames around them and at the castle. The white crystal walls only turned a dark color as fire hit them.

"Look out!" Noah yelled, pulling Mary backwards.

The two fell to the ground with a thump. Looking up they watched as the dragon crashed into the highest part of the castle and a large clump of crystal came quickly falling down to the ground only an inch from their feet.

"I thought you said these walls were unbreakable."

Mary leaned back against his chest, sitting between his legs. She stared at the large brick, shocked and thinking of how that could have been them crushed beneath it.

"I thought they were."

*****

Guards and citizens dropped dead in less than a heartbeat from the dragon who swept down, chomping them up or spitting flames at them. Thousands of tiny arrows stuck to its hide. The dragon swooped down once more, blowing flames at Gregory. He jumped out of the way but not in time as the flames charred the left side of his face.

"AHHH!"

He screamed in agony, holding his face in pain. Ripping his hands away from his face, he quickly grabbed his dagger from his side and sank it into the dragon's neck.

The dragon screeched in pain and took off flying high into the dark gloomy sky. Gregory held on to his dagger stuck in the dragon's flesh. They passed through the smoky thick cloud barrier. Smoke filled Gregory's lungs sending him into a coughing fit.

"If I die…you die with me *beast!*" Gregory croaked out his last words and used all the strength he had left to push down on the dagger slicing open its neck to its stomach.

Black blood gushed from its neck like a waterfall, pouring to the ground like rain.

The dragon fell to the ground with a loud thump. All survivors cheered seeing the beast was dead at last! But their cheering soon diminished, quickly turning to shock when they saw their king fall down seconds later.

Chapter Twelve

Noah and Mary sat in the throne room along with Jenna and all the other servants who worked in the castle. The muffled sounds of loud bangs went on for what felt like hours until…everything suddenly went still.

"Is it over?" a maid asked.

"Should we go check?" another asked.

Noah removed Mary from his lap and stood up immediately taking order.

"People…stay here…I, as the prince shall go to check if the dragon's dead."

Mary stood up next to his side. "And I will go with you."

Noah shook his head. "No…it could still be dangerous and-"

Slam!

The doors swung open, hitting the walls and almost the people nearby. Guards came piling in. Maxwell was amongst them holding something that seemed to glow in his hands. Noah looked closer as his eyes widened in a mixture of shock and pain. It was his father's crown.

"Why do you have this!" Noah ripped the heavy crown out of his hands.

"It is yours now. I am sorry, my friend."

Noah felt like he had been stabbed in the heart with multiple daggers. First his mother and now his father.

"He can't be…." Tears welled up in his eyes. He peered around at the people to see them kneeling down to their new king and bowing their heads in respect for the dead one.

"You fools! Do not kneel to me. My father is still the king."

Mary jumped at his harsh tone that boomed through the room. Hesitantly she placed a hand on his shoulder for comfort.

"Noah…."

"NO!"

He immediately regretted yelling at her, watching as she flinched back once more. Noah turned back around and walked away before stopping.

"I want everyone to clean this mess up. Start by healing the injured and…bury the dead."

***

Later that night Mary lay with her feet hanging off the bed staring up at the ceiling. She had tried to help, but Jenna stopped her seeing how much it stressed her with all the dead people around and told her to get rest. But she could not rest. She was too busy overthinking. The smell of burning flesh could not seem to leave the air, and every time Mary closed her eyes, a glimpse of bloody, blistery, burnt dead bodies stare back at her. Squeezing her eyes shut once more the dragon's yellow beady eyes appeared.

Crash!

Jumping out of her skin for the fifth time that day at a loud noise that came from the room over. Mary shot up, worrying for Noah even more than before as more bangs and stuff crashing to the ground were heard. Running out to his door, she grabbed the doorknob. Hesitantly, she opened the door only to hear another crash. Slowly she walked in, leaving the door open only a crack behind her.

This was the first time seeing his room and it was in disarray. An armor stand, knocked to the ground, five daggers lay carelessly about on the floor, one of them sticking out from a chair. Papers, quills, and ink spilled on the ground surrounding a small desk in the corner.

Noah stood in front of his king-sized bed. He wore his father's crown on top of his messy blond locks. He swung his sword at the wooden bedpost creating dents. Not knowing someone had walked in, Noah turned around throwing the metal point in Mary's direction. She ducked covering her face as it fell to the floor with a clang next to her.

"Mary…what are you doing here?"

He was almost in a daze not seeming to care that the sword almost hit her.

"I-I heard stuff breaking and I was worried."

Noah took off the crown, gripping it in his hands. Walking closer to Mary, he looked around at the mess he made.

"I…I was upset…I'm sorry I worried you."

He placed a hand under her chin, staring at her with such lust. Not love. It was almost exactly like the way Alexander stared at her. She uncomfortably shifted under his stare.

"I understand—"

"*Understand*," Noah mocked with a scoff and pulled his hand away, taking a step back. He slammed his hand on the door behind her. The loud noise echoed through the hall. Picking up his sword he walked across the room and held up his father's crown.

"This is all I have left of my father…yet I don't want it."

It was then thrown harshly to the ground. The crown landed with a loud clunk and a ruby broke off landing at Mary's feet.

"YOU DON'T UNDERSTAND! My brother hasn't been home for two years… my mother is dead…. And now so is my father. I have no one left!"

He swung his sword over and over again at the bedpost.

Bang! Slam! Bang!

With each hit, Mary flinched.

Slam! Bang! Crack!

Noah didn't even react as the thick post began to crack in half.

"Noah…calm down!" Mary exclaimed, gently gripping his arms pulling him back.

Tears fell quickly from his eyes. He limply fell to the ground in Mary's arms and sobbed loudly while taking short breaths. Mary held him close, running her fingers through his soft blond hair as he tightly gripped her dress crying into her chest.

"You haven't lost everyone. I will always be here for you." She spoke calmly, cradling him in her arms.

"I-I am s-so-sorry I yelled at yo-you," Noah managed to say through sobs.

Mary softly shushed him, saying it was alright and moved him to his bed. Lying him down on the soft comforter, she draped the silk dark green sheets over his sob-wracked body. He grabbed her wrist with a shaky hand.

"Please stay with me."

"I wasn't going anywhere," she reassured, laying down next to him. Noah turned over on his side, kissing her lips gently and pulled her close.

"Thank you."

***

The next morning Noah went with Mary to help the people clean up. They watched as the five hundred people from town roamed the burned-down area hoping to find any other survivors or possibly something of use that did not burn. The only thing left standing was rubble of cobblestone. Their valuables, homes, and families, all gone. The painting Noah was so fond of. Gone. Everything they loved. Gone forever. The people now looked to the castle to take refuge there until their homes were rebuilt.

Noah masked his sadness putting on a brave face and took long strides over to the dead dragon's large body. He stopped a few feet away as people looked on in remorse. Noah stared at the beast's body in anger and walked to the other side spotting his father's lifeless body. His once comely face was now all burnt on the one side with bloody blisters and he lay in a pool of his own blood. The dragon's black blood steamed with smoke as it mixed with Gregory's. Mary looked away as Noah grimaced at the sight walking over. He kneeled down at his father's side and closed his eyes.

"May we reunite on the other side. Rest peacefully. Tell Mother I miss her and that I love her," he whispered and then took out a pair of gloves and placed them on, taking his father's bloody sword in his hands. He walked back over to Mary's side pulling her away from the gruesome scene. Pushing past the nosey onlookers, he made sure they avoided the sword.

"It's her fault why our king is dead! The prophecy predicted this. I say we banish her," a young man shouted, riling the crowd up. Noah turned around enraged, walking up to the young man who said that. He poked his finger to the man's chest.

"We should sacrifice her and then all this madness will go away." The man dared to speak once more.

"You will keep your mouth shut if you don't want to be thrown into the dungeons!"

Noah raised his voice causing the people to grow angry at him for defending Mary. The last thing he wanted was the people of Tay to revolt against him. Lowering his tone to a calm one, Noah stepped back, pulling Mary behind him.

"Do not blame Mary for this. A prophecy is a prophecy…many more will come to light. They will be more severe and deadly than this one. Whole worlds could be destroyed."

The people listened closely and apologized but were still weary of Mary. Their words made Mary stop to think for a second. What if it was her fault? All of these innocent people. Dead because of her. Noah pulled her away and called over the head guard. Dropping the sword to the ground, he took off the gloves and handed them over to the guard.

"Put these on and place the sword to the others," he said.

"Of course, Your Majesty," the guard replied and took the sword in his gloved hands.

Noah turned back to Mary, rubbing her arm gently. "Don't listen to them…*Lye lunda*." (my love).

"What if they're right…people are dead because of me," she said, sounding upset.

"Hey.…" Noah pulled her closer and kissed her lips. "This is not your fault." he reassured her. But it didn't help too much. Mary sighed.

"I'm gonna see if Jenna needs any help," she said, kissing him on the cheek and walked off. She wandered off to find Jenna sitting on a large rock. Jenna was holding her chest, taking shaky breaths.

"Jenna…are you okay?" Mary asked worriedly and sat down next to her.

"Yes…I am fine…it is just a lot to take in," Jenna replied, smiling softly.

"Do you think this is all my fault?" Mary asked, looking back down at her feet. Jenna shook her head no, relieving her a bit from the stress of thinking this was all her fault.

They sat in silence until Jenna spoke up. "I plan on leaving tonight."

"What? No…please stay. Not for me…for Noah," Mary pleaded.

Jenna brought the young girl into her arms, hugging her tightly. "I am afraid I must go. I'm sorry."

***

Later that evening, Noah peered down into the throng of people who took refuge in the castle. There he spotted the four boys who were never too kind to him.

"Luothoring," Noah called the guard stationed nearby.

"Yes, Your Majesty?" The guard walked up to Noah bowing.

"Keep watch over those four," Noah commanded, gesturing down towards the tetrad group.

"Of course, Your Majesty. I shall inform you if they do anything."

"Yes, please do," Noah said before heading off to the front Gates of Tay.

***

"I am truly going to miss you, Jenna. You were like a second mother to me," Noah said as tears welled up in his eyes. Jenna, who already had tears streaming down her pale cheeks, pulled the boy into a hug.

"This is not the last goodbye."

"I would hope not. You are always welcome back."

Jenna let him go and turned to Mary, pulling her into a tight hug as well. "I hope you will be married by the time I visit back," she whispered, causing bright red to dust along Mary's cheeks.

"I hope so too," Mary whispered back jokingly.

She knew Jenna was only joking. Or she hoped she was only joking. Marriage was something that scared Mary. She did not want to end up like her mother and lose someone she loved dearly.

A guard soon walked out the gates pulling a stubborn horse along. The horse kept pulling back, making the guy struggle. The gentle creature seemed to not want to leave.

"Well…I should be going." Jenna said with a sad smile.

"Are you sure you do not need a guard to accompany you?" Noah asked, handing her a heavy leather purse.

"I will be fine on my own…thank you again."

"Where will you go?" Noah asked once more.

She hopped onto her horse pulling the hood of her cloak up for warmth. "I am not sure…wherever the stars lead to perhaps."

"Wait! Jenna…I have one last question to ask, but you might not know," Noah said before she could take off.

"Whatever it is…I am sure I can answer it."

Noah nodded and spoke bluntly. "Did my parents really love each other?"

Jenna looked shocked for a second until her expression turned cold.

"I don't know why you are suddenly asking that, but the king and queen loved each other."

She rode off into the night.

Noah sighed hoping he didn't upset her and pulled Mary back inside. The two walked around the large crystal block that stayed all scratched up, not moving and walked into the warmth.

"Was that a stupid question to ask?" he asked Mary as they walked down the hall.

"No…you just wanted to know…they definitely loved each other."

"Yeah…I am sure they do. It was just something I heard my mother say long ago when I was a child. Never mind," Noah said quickly, stopping before the doors of the Grand Hall. The guards on either side opened the door, releasing all the loud noise of people speaking.

"My people!" Noah held up a hand to silence them. They all quieted down bowing in respect. Some glared at the sight of Mary.

"You are welcome to stay here until your homes are rebuilt…and you are allowed to leave whenever you please…but do know that any other room besides here and the bathing rooms are restricted. The food, water, clothes, and any other supplies shall be free," Noah declared.

All people clapped and cheered, grateful for his aid. Smiling back at the happy people, he put his hand up once more to silence them. It surprised him at how fast they grew completely still. Being king gave him so much power. It almost scared him a bit.

"Tonight you shall all rest peacefully…tomorrow we mourn for the ones we lost."

Noah finished speaking and grabbed Mary's hand, turning to leave before stopping at the sound of a young woman's voice.

"We will sleep peacefully once we know that *red-haired procurer* is gone!" Her tone was laced with jealousy.

"Yeah! We could sacrifice her and all of our sorrows will diminish," another yelled out, making Mary almost fear for her life.

Noah grew angry at their harsh words and he lashed out.

"NO! You will all stop putting the blame on Mary. She is not a monster. I love her and you will all treat her the way you treat me! Because soon she will be your queen… and if anyone tries to hurt her, you will be hung for treason."

The people quickly nodded, fearing their king's harsh words and watched him protectively place Mary in front of him stomping out the doors. Mary was shocked by his sudden outburst. She understood he just wanted to scare them so they would not possibly try to hurt her. But would he really kill someone for her? Mary did not like the thought of someone's blood on her hands.

"You would not really kill them…would you?" she asked

Noah stopped before opening his door and swiftly turned to her, placing a hand on the side of her face.

"No…of course not. I just said that to scare them," he reassured her.

Mary nodded and went to leave to her room before he pulled her back closer only leaving a small gap between. She could feel his warm breath on her face as he spoke softly.

"I think it is best if you stay in my chambers for a while…that is until the people begin to trust you."

"It could be a while till they trust me." Noah kissed her lips lightly. "It doesn't matter. They could go for years not liking you. But you will be my queen soon and they will learn to like you…besides I have always wanted a roommate. It gets quite lonely," he replied suggestively with a smirk.

"Alright." Mary laughed with a bright blush. But it wasn't long till her smile faltered.

"You don't think someone is actually going to hurt me…do you?"

"I truly do not know, my love. I don't even know what I am doing as king."

Chapter Thirteen

It was true.

Noah did not know what to do or how to be a king. He only knew the basics. Plan for war, make alliances, keep order, and don't allow his virtue of power to overtake him into madness.

Without his father, though, he was lost. What else was there to such a high power? When Noah was younger, his father had his advisor Kennings give him and his brother Elliot lessons on being the king. He only paid attention to one and daydreamed through the others because he thought his brother would become the next king. He never realized how hard it was to rule a kingdom.

Kennings was a well-known man around all the kingdoms. He was a retired warrior in his fifties. Long ago the gallant soldier fought beside Noah's father and grandfather Timothe Tay the III and was Gregory's most trusted friend since they were children.

That morning Noah was woken abruptly being dragged to a council meeting. From his last experience he doubted this would go well, but it went better than he thought. Once it was over he went to rush out of the room back to Mary before she woke up. Before he could get far, though, Kennings stopped him.

"Your first meeting as king went better than I expected…your father would be proud," he said sadly, thinking of his deceased friend. Noah nodded in agreement as Kennings continued. "The next meeting will be held Friday; then we will discuss on finding your future queen to rule by your side and—"

"There will be no need for that meeting for I have found my queen," Noah interrupted, wearing a loving smile. Kennings sighed.

"Lady Mary is not of royal blood. She is not even from here. Don't you want to create an alliance with other kingdoms? I know of a few lords from overseas who desperately want an alliance with the greatest kingdom in Lotogettar."

"I do not care what other lords want. So what if Mary is not of 'royal blood?' My father told me to marry for love…and that is what Mary and I have."

Noah wore a determined look. He refuses to marry some lord's daughter he never met before. If he could not have Mary, he would give up his crown and leave the kingdom of Tay without a second glance.

"You remind me a lot of myself when I was younger. And don't forget to write that letter," Kennings said, wearing a soft smile. He patted Noah on the back and left.

Noah stood there thinking over all the past events and grabbed a blank piece of paper and quill, dipping it twice in the ink. He began to write quickly and read aloud.

"Dear brother…I am truly sorry for the late notice, but so much tragedy has happened and I am sure you heard the rumors…that both our parents are gone. The dragon that was once caged, broke free killing tons of civilians…homes destroyed… even a part of crystal from our home broke. I am now king…and do not know what to do. We call for help from Plake Kingdom to help rebuild the town and fight a war that our uncle started. I hope to see you soon…your brother Noah Tay…King of Tay."

Noah sealed the letter with melted green wax stamping it down with the Tay house symbol. He ran out the library doors, stopping a guard walking by.

"Quickly take this to Plake Kingdom," Noah ordered and handed him the letter.

"Of course, Your Majesty." The guard bowed and rushed off.

***

The funerals of all that died from the flames of the beast, were held that afternoon. They were all held in the graveyard just outside the castle gates behind the gardens.

Children gripped on to their mothers' skirts crying for the loss of their fathers. Husbands and wives held each other close sobbing for the loss of their children.

Once it was over, they migrated to the gardens where the king lay on a stone slab, surrounded by flowers. He would be buried next to where the queen was buried.

"*Guasaf keen kansiy!*" The people yelled out, kneeling down to their new king and deceased one before heading off back into the castle.

"What did that mean?" Mary asked.

"It means the old king is dead…long live the new one," Noah replied and walked up to his father. He pulled a silk blanket over his father. He no longer wanted to see the horrific burns on his father's face. Noah sniffled, wiping away a tear and pulled Mary towards the castle.

"Come along…it's cold out here."

***

Knock! Knock! Knock!

Mary sighed leaning back into Noah's chest. "Can't we watch the stars peacefully?" She pulled her cloak closer for warmth. Noah chuckled and gently kissed her cheek.

"Do not fret *lye lunda*…we will have many more nights like this."

He turned to walk back into the room. Mary went to follow before he stopped her.

"Stay here. We don't want anyone to spread rumors…now do we?" Noah whispered in the shell of her ear.

"Rumors?" She raised an eyebrow questionably. "Everyone already knows where together, though."

"Yes but…we're not supposed to share a room until we are betrothed, and the people of Tay would feed into such a…*carnal scandal.*" He raised a brow suggestively. Mary laughed, slapping his chest lightly as two more short impatient knocks came from the door.

"I'll be right back," Noah said, running to the door.

He swung it open to reveal the guard he sent off yesterday morning.

"Your Majesty." He bowed and handed him a letter. "From your brother."

Noah took it happily in his hands looking down at the blue sealed letter. Noah looked up, meeting the guard's tired eyes. Guilt suddenly washed over the young king feeling bad for rushing him that morning.

"You have served me well today. You shall be free from all your duties for the rest of the night."

The guard thanked him greatly for letting him rest after such a long day and left. Noah closed the door and walked back on the balcony to Mary's side.

"What's that?" Mary asked, leaning her head on his shoulder.

"It's a letter from my brother."

He was wearing a giddy smile and opened it up reading aloud.

"Dear brother, King of Tay

I have heard the rumors…but hoped they were not true. I meant to write, but it was hard to find time when I am free. I miss you…and mother and father. I wish you had told me sooner. Though I should have known the prophecy would play out sooner and this would happen. You are king now, do not be afraid…don't show weakness. I have asked the King of Plake to send immediate help to Tay. Five thousand soldiers shall arrive in one day at sunrise. I will accompany them over to Tay.

Sincerely your brother, Elliot."

Noah could not hide his childish smile and embraced Mary, burying his head into the crook of her neck, His breath tickling her skin.

"Maybe things are going to get a lot better."

"Maybe they are." Mary hoped.

"Let us go to bed…*lye lunda*. We need to wake up early for my brother's arrival," Noah said, pulling her over to his bed, collapsing down with her in his arms.

***

"Where are they? They should have been here an hour ago. Plake Kingdom is only one day's journey away." Noah sighed with frustration.

That morning just as soon as the sun rose, Noah tugged Mary out of bed, giving her only enough time to wrap her cloak around her white silk nightgown. Since then they had stood out by the gates heavily guarded by soldiers.

"Maybe they are just running a little late. They might have changed to arriving in the afternoon. Maybe we should go inside and wait," Mary tried to reason.

"Let's just wait a few more seconds," he implored.

Almost another hour went by as they stood shivering in the freezing cold. Still waiting…and waiting…and more waiting. Mary sighed and moved in front of Noah.

"We can't stand out here all day. What if they arrive at night?"

He huffed out a frustrated stubborn sigh.

"Fine. If you want to keep complaining…then go inside…but I am going to stay out here and wait till night if I have to."

Mary was taken aback by his tone. He sounded so irritated with her and did not even acknowledge her hurt expression as he stared straight over her head.

"I'm sorry for annoying you." She spoke bitterly and pushed him gently aside, walking away with her head down.

Noah came back to reality and grabbed her wrist. "Wait…I am sorry. I had not meant to sound so impolite."

"It's…alright." Mary sighed. She always forgave people too easily.

"My love…you forgive too straightforwardly. What if I hurt you from my harsh words? What if I hit—"

She quickly stood on her tippy toes. planting a chaste kiss on his lips to quiet him.

"Don't worry…You could never hurt me," she whispered against his lips. He pulled away and held her close, placing his head on top of hers.

"You are too good for me," he murmured.

"*Shor Quelental!* There is an army approaching the kingdom," (Your Majesty) a guard warned from the towers above the gates. Noah's demeanor changed fast to an exultant mood. Looking out to the field, he saw a decent-sized army.

"My brother is home!" Noah shouted.

He began to run out to them. Though as he grew closer his smile faltered and hurriedly he came to a halt.

Chapter Fourteen

The flags that were held high above whipping through the strong wind were not Plake's blue lion ones. This was not his brother leading an army of Plake soldiers. This was his cousin, King Alexander Caesar. He did not deserve such a title after the way he treated Mary. The thoughts disgusted him about what Alexander is capable of and what would have happened if he had not stopped him.

Noah hurriedly stumbled to the ground, feeling the dried grass between his hands. He immediately felt like a craven. Falling to the ground. Weak. No weapons to bear or armor to wear. He stood up quickly and ran back to Mary's side, pushing her behind him to shield her from Alexander's view.

"Guards! Stand quick," Noah commanded.

Guards piled out beside him readying their weapons and holding out their shields. Maxwell ran out to his friend's side, handing Noah a sword and chainmail. Slipping the heavy chains over his flowy white shirt he held his sword tightly and put on a blood-thirsty look.

Alexander and his army stopped within twenty-five feet of Noah and his army.

Noah tightened his grip on his sword as he glared up at his cousin who sat prideful on top of his horse. He wore great robes of silk and bear fur. Lying perfectly over his blond hair was his father's golden crown.

"My cousin! Good to see you again. I love what you've done with the place," he said sarcastically, looking around to see no village and a missing chunk of the castle.

"Why did you come back? Last I heard you and your army fled like foolish cowards when you heard the mere roar of a dragon." Noah laughed.

Alexander scoffed and hopped off his horse. "Now now…there is no need to raise your weapons at me," he continued with a smile.

"I have come to make an agreement I—" He stopped short. A disgusted look fell upon his face as a gust of wind blew past him. *"Disgusting!* What is that horrid smell?" he asked, holding his nose.

"That's burning flesh. It is nothing new here in Tay. If you haven't noticed we lost people to dragon—"

"Yes…oh well," Alexander interrupted carelessly and continued. "As I said before, I have come to negotiate a trade deal…to avoid war of course."

Noah sighed, aggravated by his cousin's nonsense.

"What is it you want? Money? Because I have plenty of it."

"No…no. I have plenty of money as well. What I want is behind you."

Mary's heart dropped at Alexander's words.

"There is nothing behind me."

Noah lied growing angry. He would not just trade Mary like she was a lamb.

"I know she's behind you. I can see her fiery hair from a mile away. Mary come out. Do not hide from me," Alexander replied.

Noah took Mary's hand in his as she stepped out moving next to Noah's side, just glaring at him. Alexander tilted his head mockingly and spoke smoothly.

"Oh…how beautiful. It is good to see you again and I must tell you…ever since I've set my eyes on you I have grown very fond of you." Alexander took his eyes off Mary to look at his cousin. "If we make a trade with you for her…we could avoid war," he concluded.

Noah guffawed at him.

"I will have you know that Mary is my love…and I would never trade her even if it were to save the whole world of Lotogettar itself from being destroyed. You are foolish to think I would just trade her away like a whore," he said with anger filling his tone.

"I knew you would say that. But you would not even do it for someone who was like a second mother to you?"

Alexander raised a brow with a grin on his face. Two guards were motioned to come forth. They walked out front next to their king, pulling someone along as their bare white feet dragged behind them. The hostage they had captured was a woman. Her long brown hair was matted and her dress was torn apart. The woman's face was bloodied and bruised.

Mary and Noah both echoed each other's hurt gasps.

"Jenna!"

"She was a lot of fun for my soldiers…they got a bit out of hand. I was going to join them but you see I am…saving that for Mary," Alexander said as his lustful eyes roamed Mary's body. She shifted uncomfortably. She grew sick to her stomach, setting her eyes on Jenna. Tears began to well up in her eyes.

The soldiers threw Jenna's weak frail body to the ground with smirks upon their disgusting faces.

"M-Mary…st-stay back…," Jenna wheezed as Mary went to rush to her aid.

Noah quickly grabbed Mary back into his arms before she could get any farther, restraining her from running out again.

"Looks like Mary wants to make the trade. You have one minute to decide."

A tear fell down Noah's cheek as he met Jenna's tired eyes.

"Don't do it," she managed to say.

"Quiet you!" Alexander yelled as the guard pulled Jenna up by her hair. Mary gasped as tears rushed down her face. She squirmed in Noah's arms desperately wanting to get Jenna.

"No please! LET HER GO!"

"Too late! I shall make the decision for you," Alexander sneered as the soldier made his move lifting his sword high in the air. The metal blade swung down slicing her head clean off.

"NOOO!" Mary cried out.

Noah pulled her head into his chest preventing her from seeing the gruesome scene of Jenna's headless body falling to the ground. The guard dropped her head making it roll all the way to Noah's feet.

The world around him began to spin when he looked down at Jenna's bloody head. Her lifeless brown eyes stared back at his blue ones. Noah stumbled back with Mary still firmly in his arms. Looking Alexander directly in his eyes he could have sworn he saw a glint of guilt in them.

"How could you…why would…?"

Noah stumbled over his words. He turned around, pushing through the line of guards.

"KILL THEM! Kill them all. I don't want to see any of them living!" Noah ordered his soldiers.

"Chaaaarge!"

The Tay army pointed their swords towards the cloudy sky, letting battle cries erupt from their mouths. The Caesar army mirrored their actions and began to charge.

Alexander stood there in fear watching both armies trampling over Jenna's body, colliding together. He fled the scene running to hide behind the side of the castle walls.

Noah took Mary through the gates of the castle bringing her to a watchtower. Opening the wooden door, he pushed Mary in.

"Mary you need to stay here. I will come get you when this is over. Lock yourself in," he said through tears and handed her a wooden slab. Mary dropped the wood carelessly and jumped back into his arms, tightening her hold on him.

"Please don't go…please don't leave me."

"I have to fight…I will come back…I promise. I love you."

He kissed her lovingly one last time and shut the door between them. All light in the small room faded away.

"I love you too."

She mumbled leaning her back against the door sliding to the ground.

On the outside Noah twirled his sword in his hand running out into the battlefield to fight the final battle. He made his way through the crowd of soldiers. The Tay soldiers were cutting their way through the Caesar fighters fast. Noah blocked the blades coming his way immediately swinging his sword at the enemies' throats.

He listened satisfied as the men were heard choking on their own blood.

"AHH—"

Turning around he pierced his sword through an enemy's leather red chest plate. The tall man fell to the ground. Noah looked into his lifeless eyes with no remorse. Looking up he saw Maxwell. A line of blood splattered along his face as he sliced a man's neck open.

"Look out!"

Noah shouted running forward to pierce his sword through the Caesar soldier who snuck up behind his friend. Maxwell turned around stunned.

"I almost just died," he breathed.

"Yes, you did…go guard the gates. Do not let anyone get through and do not let anyone leave."

Noah commanded and went off swinging his sword down at anybody who crossed his path in search of his cousin.

Meanwhile Mary sat on the floor holding her knees to her chest. Swords clanging against each other could be faintly heard from outside. Mary sighed, trying to take her mind off Jenna. closing her eyes she began to stress as horrible thoughts began to shift through her mind. *Will Noah really be safe? What if he doesn't keep his promise? What if—?*

SLAM!

Mary broke from her thoughts as something hit the door. She jumped up and gripped the wooden slab that barricaded the door.

Should I open it? What if it's Noah…and he's hurt, she thought.

Hesitantly pushing off the wood barricade and slowly opening the door Mary peeked her head out. She peered around and looked down to see Maxwell knocked out with a gash on his head.

Mary gasped, leaning down to his side. She took her shaky hand, pressing two fingers to his neck checking for a pulse. It was still there but very weak.

Mary stood back up only to be shoved down once more. Turning around a sword swung in her direction and she impishly gripped the cold sharp blade. She hissed in pain and pulled her hand back clutching it to her chest. The redhead turned back to Maxwell and went to grab his sword for protection but before she could make another move a blade was pressed against her neck. A shaky breath escaped her mouth as panic set in.

"You're the pretty thing the king is looking for…get up!" a deep voice growled.

She didn't move.

"Did you hear me? I said—"

The man stopped quickly, gripping his throat as a gurgle escaped through his lips.

Blood splattered on Mary's face as he fell to the ground by her side. Mary gasped, looking down at Maxwell's sword now in her hands. Blood dripped from the end of it. Mary killed the man. She looked down at the stranger's dead blue eyes. Surprised at her own actions she stood up, dropping the sword to the ground.

Not wanting to touch it again, Mary kicked the sword to Maxwell's side and left him, hoping he would be fine and ran out to the gates. But she stopped short, witnessing the huge battle unfolding before her eyes.

Blood splattered everywhere as men slashed at each other's throats, arms and legs. Limbs broken off from bodies lay there like nothing. Men crying out in agony and retching on their own blood. The disturbing sounds and images made her want to throw up. She never thought she would ever see a real battle happening before her eyes.

Mary never wanted to witness the last thing her father had to be a part of, but here she was. Continuing on, running in a safe distance of not having to get her head chopped off she looked for Noah. Knowing it was a stupid decision.

The red-haired girl went unnoticed by all except one. Mary's adrenaline kicked in as she spotted Noah's head of blond locks and began running to him. Managing to avoid the swords that swung her way. Growing closer to him she went to yell out his name before someone jumped in front of her.

"AHHH!"

Mary jumped back, looking to see Alexander.

"Mary…do not be afraid," he breathed out and took a step closer to her.

"Stay away from me," Mary said with fear lacing her voice.

"Please…I love you."

It almost sounded as if he were begging her to love him back. As he took more steps closer, she could see the obsession flashing through his eyes as he looked her up and down.

Each step he took closer, she took one more back farther. One more step almost inches away, Mary ran off. Alexander ran after her with a furious look upon his face.

Mary ran as fast as she could. Her heart pumped hard and quick against her chest. Mary took a glance back to see Alexander right on her tail. They were growing farther and farther away from the battle. Glancing back once more Mary tripped over her feet and fell to the ground with a thud. Alexander jumped down on her, pinning her to the ground, and trapping her between his legs. Mary turned around squirming in his grip, trying to get loose.

"NOAH! HELP—" Before she could yell another word, he covered her mouth.

"Shh! Shut up…shut up!"

Mary freed her arm and pressed her injured bloody hand to his face. She pulled away as pain coursed up her arm. A bloody handprint left on his white skin.

"Stop fighting—who did this to you?" Alexander's demeanor changed from irritation to concern. He grabbed her wrist examining her cut watching as blood leaked down her arm.

"Come back to my kingdom with me…I'll heal you. We could be together…my love," he said kissing her injury not caring if he got blood on his lips. He kept his other hand over her mouth, preventing her from yelling.

The boy who could pass at being Noah's twin was so in love with Mary. So desperate to be with her. He would not let her go. Not when he just caught her, ready to take her home.

"You can be a queen. My queen…we can learn to love each other."

He released his hand from her pink lips and in a quick motion he roughly kissed them. Mary squirmed, pressing her hands against his hard chest. But immediately regretted it as her hand coursed in pain.

"Get off her!"

Someone yelled, kicking him in the side and away from Mary. Scrambling back on her elbows she looked up at Noah standing over her. Alexander regained himself and stood up. He unsheathed his sword and swung at Noah. Noah swung back. Both kings connected swords with loud clangs that echoed through the field, directly over Mary's head.

"How dare you put your filthy hands on my woman!" Noah snapped, swinging his sword upwards along with Alexander's. All the while Mary blocked her arms in front of her afraid to get hit.

"Your woman," Alexander scoffed and brought his sword down to slice open Noah's arm before being blocked.

"Yes…mine." Noah kicked his cousin to the ground moving swiftly with his sword pressed to his throat. "Give me one good reason why I should not kill you right here… right now."

Alexander swallowed thickly. "I—ack!" He gagged as the tip of the sword pressed harder, drawing a line of blood. Noah relaxed his grip to let him continue. "We're cousins!"

Noah scoffed, raising his sword high above his head. "Not good enough."

He brought the sword down to lop off Alexander's head.

Mary squeezed her eyes shut, waiting to hear the sickening noise of a head to be chopped off. But it never came. She opened her eyes to see Alexander dodging each swing of Noah's sword only inches from his head.

"Wait. WAIT! Please just hear me out!"

Swinging his sword once last time, Alexander gave up cowering in fear. The sword met the ground digging deep into the dirt.

"You are pathetic," Noah spat coldly.

"I am sorry for ordering that guard to kill Jenna…and—oh goodness." Alexander stopped short wearing an unreadable expression. "I have become my father," he said under his breath.

Noah's irate demeanor changed to remorse. His cousin, once his best friend, now sat in front of him scared of what he had become. Noah felt bad for his cousin. He had to live with his father's harsh past on his shoulders. But Noah also knew his cousin was blinded by his father's corrupt insanity. He also knew he was blinded by love.

"I told you to stay in the watchtower!"

The war was now over. The very few Caesar soldiers that survived were chained and locked in the dungeons along with their king.

Noah was pacing back and forth in the healing room as Mary got her hand wrapped with bandages. She told him she was fine and it was nothing to worry about, but he insisted she go straight to the healing room.

"You would not have gotten hurt if you stayed there! I should murder him for what he did. He had Jenna killed. You got hurt because of him…and he kissed you!"

Noah was unable to control his anger as he yelled out walking back and forth in the healing room. He immediately regretted snapping at Mary. The poor young nurse wrapping the bandages around Mary's hand jumped every time he raised his voice.

"She is all healed *Shor quelental*," (Your Majesty) the nurse said quietly and raced out of the room.

Noah sighed sitting down on the small bed next to her.

"Noah, it's okay," she reassured him. But it wasn't okay. Mary could still feel Alexander's lips on hers.

"It is not okay! Only I can kiss you," he replied gently, gripping her chin. Tilting her head upwards. "It is not okay. I promise he won't touch you ever again."

Mary closed her eyes as he pressed a passionate kiss to her lips. Suddenly an image appeared in her mind. Not a good one. She tensed up and pulled away.

Noah frowned. "What's wrong?"

She smiled reassuringly.

"Nothing."

***

Disgusting remarks were thrown at Mary as both her and Noah walked through the dungeons. One man even reached his arm out through the crystal cell bars trying to grab Mary. Noah glared at the man.

"*Apolenge hik!*" (silence him!) he ordered and pulled Mary protectively in front of him.

The guards walking behind them stopped. They opened the cell door and held the man down while the other punched him.

Mary gasped and turned back, watching as spit and blood flew off the man's face with each punch thrown at him.

"Do not look," Noah whispered.

He placed his hand on her cheek, moving it gently back forward and moved his hand to her arms guiding her farther through the dungeons. Inappropriate insults were still being thrown back and forth. Mary uncomfortably shifted hugging her arms around her stomach trying to block out all noise around her. They neared the cell where Alexander was being held.

"You owe Mary an apology," Noah declared, staring coldly at his cousin who sat in a cramped cell.

His hands were shackled and he was sitting against the wall with his head in his hands. Mary met his blue eyes once he lifted his head. She was no longer mad at him. She felt bad for him.

"Mary…I am truly sorry and if you can…please forgive me. I should have never kissed you." His voice was raspy as he spoke with guilt. He then turned to Noah.

"I am sorry, Noah. We used to be such good friends. My father did not like that, so he told me that I do not need any friends, saying it made me look weak and that when I was king one day they would turn against me. So I believed him. I thought maybe if I pushed you away, it would not hurt me later in the future when you would abandon me. I hope someday we can be a family again."

Noah sighed, still a bit irritated. "It will take me a while to forgive and trust you."

"I understand," Alexander mumbled, nodding along with every word.

"Your Majesty! Your brother has arrived with seven hundred Plake soldiers…they await you in the throne room." Maxwell came into view speaking quickly.

Noah would have put on a happy smile if he weren't so upset with his cousin. He nodded and looked back to his cousin who sat there like a hopeless mess. The guards that beat up the man who was eyeing Mary from before came back to their king's side.

"Give me the keys to the cells."

The guards gave a short nod and tossed over a ring of twenty keys. Noah took one key smaller than the others pushing it into the keyhole. Alexander leaped forward gripping the cold bars. The door unlocked with a click. Alexander stumbled out as Noah swung the cell door open and held up his shackled hands.

"You have one night to prove to me I can trust you."

Noah unlocked his cuffed hands. Alexander rubbed his wrists to relieve the pain as the heavy cuffs fell to the ground.

"Get my cousin here a room. There will be a feast held tonight. Escort him down to attend and until then do not let him leave the room," Noah said

He handed him over to Maxwell.

"What? Oh come on! I heard Elliot was here…can't I at least say hello?" Alexander was visibly annoyed while Maxwell pulled him away. Noah ignored him and followed them out with Mary at his side. Reaching the top of the long stairs and locking the door behind him Noah pulled Mary to his chest, dismissing his two guards.

"My love…what's wrong? You have been tense from the moment we came inside. Is it Alexander? Because if so I can send him straight back to the dungeons."

Mary shook her head.

"No it's not that…it's really nothing."

"Please tell me what is wrong," Noah begged, caressing his thumb against her cheek.

She sighed. "During the battle a man came running at me saying he was gonna take me to Alexander…I panicked and I…I killed him." Tears welled up in her eyes. She could still see the sword sinking through his skin and hear him choking on his own blood.

"You did what you had to do. If you did not, there is a possibility you might not have been in my arms right now." Noah brought her into a hug and continued. "There's no need to worry. One less bad man we have to deal with in the world. Now come along, my love. My brother would love to meet you."

Chapter Fifteen

"Tanha!" (Brother!)

Noah swung open the doors to the throne room rushing in with Mary at his side. Elliot stood talking with a few Plake soldiers who were dressed in metal armor that had a glint of blue. The older Tay sibling stopped his conversation, turning around to face his brother wearing a calm yet jubilant expression.

"Tanha! Barmar quenal." (Brother! Good to see you again.)

Walking up to his brother, he pulled him into a tight hug. Elliot was much taller than Noah and looked exactly like Gregory with his brown hair that landed just above his shoulders.

"By the look of outside, it seems we arrived a little late…so sorry."

"It is alright. I am just glad to see you after so long."

Noah pulled away and stared at the thin white crystal circlet on top of his head. It was similar to Noah's when he was prince.

"You should be wearing this instead of me," Noah said, motioning to their father's crown that sat on top of his head. "You are father's firstborn."

Elliot dismissed him, patting his back. "Nonsense. Now tell me…why is our cousin locked up?" His voice was rich and deep as he spoke. He glanced at Mary for a quick second, sending her a dashing smile.

"Our cousin was locked up and taken prisoner along with the few Caesar soldiers that were left. I did this because they killed Jenna…and he kissed the one I love without

her consent. Though as of now I allowed him to be a "free man" under mine and my guards' watch."

Elliot nodded along to his younger brother's every word. His expression was sad, learning of Jenna's death. She was like a second mother to him.

"We shall hold a ceremony for Jenna tomorrow."

Elliot nodded and turned to Mary. "Is this *'the one you love'*?"

"Yes...this is Mary," Noah answered, staring at her lovingly.

"Lady Mary...it is a pleasure to meet the woman who stole my brother's heart. I am Elliot." He bowed before her, taking her hand in his and placing a gentle kiss on the back. A pink crimson dusted over her cheeks.

"It is nice to meet you as well. Noah told me all about you."

"Good things I hope."

Elliot sent her one last charming smile before turning to his brother with a grin.

"*Hinalan tanha! Sho seaik shorelf a wayleta bea.*" (Congratulations, brother! You found yourself a *beautiful* lady.)

Noah glared at his brother as he emphasized the word *beautiful*.

Laughing aloud Elliot patted his brother on the shoulder.

"*Wentail bi sal shellom...sho darol imale lunda fita anome wayleta bea.*" (Do not be so jealous. You know I am in love with another beautiful woman)

"*Darno shellom!*" (I am not jealous!) Noah defended.

"Oh sure...I shall see you both later at the feast." Elliot dismissively waved him off and left the room chuckling to himself.

"Come along, my love. Let us go take a stroll through the gardens before we get ready for the feast," Noah suggested, wrapping an arm around Mary's shoulder and guiding her out to the gardens.

They took slow steps walking down a path with large white pillars and pink and white roses wrapped around them. The sun was now setting and the air was silent and cold. Mary wandered away from Noah's side as they stepped into the gazebo. She leaned on a pillar, gazing out at the sky as it slowly turned darker shades. A freezing breeze whooshed past her. Mary shivered, clutching her cloak.

"It's getting colder. We should head back—" Mary stopped short with a gasp as she turned back around to see Noah was down on one knee. Mary walked forward, holding a hand to her mouth.

"Mary...." He grabbed her hand gently, pressing a kiss to her knuckles. "Ever since I found you in the forest, I knew you were meant for me. I am so lucky to have such a beautiful woman like you with me and now I ask you...*lye lunda*...will you marry me."

Noah pulled out a ring with a golden band and a crystal diamond that glowed a faint blue when it was rotated only just a bit.

Mary felt her whole body shake from shock as she stared down at his hopeful smile. If she said yes she would be by his side forever.

Forever

The word echoed in her head.

What if she lost him and would end up like her mother? Would she ever see her mother again? Or her aunt? What about Max…?

Would Mary even go home? She never thought of it until now.

No words were able to come from Mary's mouth. Only a stutter.

"Uh-I-I…I-sorry."

Mary turned on her heels and began quickening her pace away from Noah.

"WAIT!" Noah shouted, capturing her in his arms before she could get far.

"I am sorry if that was too fast. We have only known each other for a whole month. I understand if you do not want to marry me." He dolefully frowned.

Mary turned around still stuck in his arms and stared into his sad blue eyes. It made her sad. She could not just run from him. *She loved him*. She then realized that home was long gone. Lotogettar was her new one.

"Okay."

"What was that?" he asked anxiously.

Smiling brightly she responded louder, "Yes! I'll marry you."

Noah's nerves went away and he pulled her tightly against his chest. He tilted her head upwards, barely any room between them and captured her lips in a kiss. Noah delicately pinned her to the crystal pillar behind them and deepened their kiss.

"I love you," he whispered against her lips.

Gently he slipped the sparkling white gem onto her index finger. Mary looked at him confused.

"I think you put it on the wrong finger."

"In Tay tradition we put the ring on your pointer finger to show that you are betrothed…then once we are to wed, I will switch your ring to your ring finger." He placed another passionate kiss on her lips. "Come along, let us go get ready for the feast. We can announce the wonderful news to everyone."

The two ran across the trimmed grass back towards the castle. Mary came to a quick halt, pulling Noah into her arms.

"I love you."

She kissed his lips softly.

Pulling away they looked up to see small white flurries falling from the dusk sky. Holding out her bare hand Mary watched the cold tiny dots melt away as they hit her warm skin. Noah sighed with contentment, hugging Mary from behind and brought his lips down to the shell of her ear whispering, "Nothing can ruin this perfect day."

***

Later at the feast Noah and Mary sat with Elliot at the grand table. In front of them were four long wide tables that were lower to the ground than theirs. All the people from town sat eating happily with all the great foods that they hadn't had before.

One by one the people passed by their new king bowing and thanking him greatly for his hospitality. And though nobody could see due to the long green tablecloths. Noah was holding Mary's hand in his, gently drawing patterns of circles in the palm of her hand.

Everyone but Elliot was clueless of their weird behavior. Noah thought he was being sly with the winks and smirks he kept sending Mary all through their meal.

A soft smile granted Elliot's lips. He had only just met the ginger and already adored her, seeing how she made his brother happy.

As everyone continued eating they were suddenly interrupted. The doors swung open and in walked Maxwell escorting Alexander over to his seat next to Elliot. He was all cleaned now and no longer had Mary's blood on his lips. The room grew quiet as Alexander made it to his seat and sat tense feeling eyes all over him. If looks could kill, he would have thousands of daggers shoved in his face.

"TRAITOR!" people began shouting out at him.

Noah leaned back in his cushioned chair, holding up a hand to silence everyone.

"My people…I understand the mistake my cousin has made, but I have decided to forgive him and allow him a chance to redeem his reputation. We all deserve second chances." The people hesitantly nodded with a few irritated grumbles under their breaths. "On the other hand, I have an important announcement to make," he added with a twinkle in his eyes as he stood up. He revealed his hand holding Mary's with pride. "I would like to announce that Mary has agreed to be my wife and future Queen of Tay!"

And instead of disagreeing and causing a scene, their hard cold glares softened. They saw how much he really loved her. Elliot stood up with a proud smile, holding his chalice high in the air as everyone did the same.

"To Mary and Noah's betrothal! May they be blessed with a long, happy life together." Elliot turned to the two.

"I am proud of you, brother…and welcome to the family, Mary."

Everyone quieted down, having small conversations with each other. They were starting to accept Mary, sending small smiles her way. All the people but one were happy with this news.

Alexander.

His emotions all bubbled up at once. Upset that he did not get to Mary first. If only he had met her before his cousin. It wasn't fair. *Noah gets everything he wants.* A loud shaky breath was heard from his lips. He stood up quickly, almost knocking over his chalice filled with wine.

Elliot frowned at his cousin's behavior as he began to walk off. If he was being honest he thought Alexander should still be in a cell. His actions only made him more mad with his cousin. Alexander should be happy for Noah and Mary.

"Where are you going?" Elliot asked, grabbing ahold of his shoulder.

"None of your business!" Alexander said and harshly shoved his hand off, walking through the exit.

"What is his problem?" Elliot asked, turning to his brother.

Noah scoffed. His happy mood now turned sour. "He is just jealous, that's all. I will bring him back." Noah went to stand up before Mary stopped him.

"Let me talk to him."

"I don't know if that is such a good idea," Noah disagreed.

"He will listen to me," Mary said and went after Alexander.

Noah watched anxiously as she left. He did not trust Mary alone with his cousin. In fact he did not trust anyone alone with her. Noah did not want to see her hurt or worse.

"I have a bad feeling about this. I will be back," Noah whispered to his brother and quickly followed after her.

Walking along a narrow hallway Mary came to a door that was just a crack open. Pushing it fully open, Mary stepped out to reveal she was now on the outside of the giant walls that barricaded the castle. Out in the open. No longer safe.

Peering around her surroundings, she did not see any sign of Alexander. Only a soft white blanket of snow that reached far across the lands.

The cold wind blew past. She pulled her arms around herself for warmth, shivering as the wind picked up, blowing her red locks in her face. Mary cursed herself for not grabbing her cloak. All she had on was a green dress that flowed with the wind and short sleeves.

"Alexander!" She shouted hoping he was out here. "Alexander! Where are—Ahhmph!"

Someone covered her mouth from behind, preventing her from continuing to yell out. Alexander came into view when she was turned around. He pressed his chest to hers. Slowly he removed his hand from her mouth. Before his breath could hit her face she harshly shoved him away.

"What the hell!" Mary yelled.

Noah watched from around the corner deciding if he should intervene or not.

"What's your problem!"

Alexander walked closer with each step she took back. Just like he had before during the battle. He started to tear up and guffawed at her remark.

"*My problem.*" He seethed, backing her into the wall. She was cornered and there was no point in running away. "Your '*important announcement*' that my cousin made is the problem!" he roared loudly, punching the hard crystal beside her head. She covered her face in fear she would be his next target.

Noah's anger flamed and he immediately went to Mary's protection.

"HEY!"

Alexander swiftly turned to face his cousin as tears streamed down his face.

"Oh no…no you stay there. You get everything that comes your way.…It is not fair!" he sneered and continued to wail, pointing to himself. "My whole life I have never got to feel what it was like to be loved…and when I met Mary, I had hope that maybe… just maybe she would fall in love with me…AND I STILL HAVE HOPE!"

"You are filling your head with all these fantasies! You just can't get over the fact that she will never love you!"

Those words sunk deep in Alexander's chest. It hurt him badly. He clasped a hand over his mouth suspending a sob. "Maybe you're right.… If I cannot have her…then neither can you."

Stab! …

It all happened so fast. Alexander did not even know what he had done as he dug the dagger deep into her stomach and pulled it out. Alexander came back to reality watching as her blood dripped down the metal point, falling onto the snow.

"What have I done?" Alexander muttered.

His eyes wide with shock. He dropped the dagger from his shaky hands.

"No no no no no," he kept repeating under his breath. Only hoping this was all just a bad dream.

In a quick second Noah leaped forward beyond furious. Knocking Alexander to the ground, he gripped his tunic with one hand to keep him steady while the other pounded his face over and over again. Alexander was dazed and weak as blood flew off from his face. At this point Noah did not care if he killed his cousin. He raised his fist once more to take the final punch but stopped at the sound of Mary's weak voice.

"N-Noah, please…," she wheezed, clutching her stomach and wincing as blood gushed from her wound.

Mary swayed on her feet. All she could feel was the agonizing pain in her stomach. She pressed down on the gash, hoping it would stop the blood. But it didn't. It only grew worse. Noah ran to her side, catching her just before she was inches away from hitting the snowy ground. The red sticky liquid covered her hand. She pulled it away from her stomach to reveal the open wound.

"HELP! SOMEBODY H-help me…!" Noah shouted. Tears rolled down his cheeks as he continued to call out desperately for help. He held her in a tight embrace not caring if blood stained his white cloak and green robes. Mary smiled softly up at him.

"This is it…this was my dream."

She placed her bloody hand on his cheek.

"What do you mean…my love?"

"I-it is nothing…here."

Mary moved her hand down to her hair, unclipping the hairclip that Jenna gifted her. Her arm felt heavy as she placed it in Noah's hand. He slipped it into his pocket and took her cold hand in his warm one.

"Mary…I love you. I am going to get you healed, alright? And you will be better than ever."

"I love you too…but you know that is not true."

Her head felt heavy, allowing it to fall back limply as she took a shaky breath.

"Do not say that! Please, you're going to be alright. Okay?"

"Okay…," she slurred.

Noah held her head back up and leaned down. He held his trembling lips to hers. Even when he closed his eyes his tears broke through falling onto her face.

"*Shor quelental!*" (*Your Majesty*)

Noah released his lips from hers and glanced at his guards. They held their swords out on alert but soon lowered them at the sight of their future queen laying in the king's arms.

"Brother what—oh my…."

Elliot came running out with Maxwell at his side.

"Mary?" Maxwell asked, hoping his eyes deceived him and that she was fine.

Noah looked towards Alexander's unconscious figure.

"Take him back to the dungeons…he shall be hanged in a month's time."

His eyes drifted over to the bloody dagger that lay a few feet away in the snow.

"How did he come by a dagger? WHO GAVE HIM A DAMN DAGGER!?"

The air grew quiet. No one knew what to say. They only took a step back, shocked at their king's sudden outburst. Only one person was brave enough to step forward.

"That would be my dagger…I am truly sorry my friend…I must have not noticed he snuck it off me."

Tears welled up in his eyes. Noah stared at his friend with such hatred. He felt *betrayed*.

"Go. Turn in your weapons and leave this kingdom."

"But Noah—"

"GO! NEVER RETURN."

Maxwell felt a sting in his heart. His breaths became unsteady. Both of his friends got hurt and it was all his fault. He sped back into the castle upset, getting ready to pack and take his leave.

Noah turned back to Mary. Her face was pale and her eyes were closed. "Mary?"

Noah shook her a bit, causing her head to slump back. Her shaky breaths were no longer heard.

"Mary? Come on…wake up!"

He shook her roughly and desperately trying to wake her back up. He was convinced that she would wake up and be okay.

"Come on…we're going to heal you and you're going to be okay…we just need you to wake up. When you're better…we are going to have a big wedding…we're going to have a family. Come on, please! I have lost too many already…I cannot lose you as well." His voice cracked as he continued to shake her. Elliot walked over to his brother's hunched-over form and placed a hand on his shoulder.

"Noah, stop. I am so sorry but…she's—"

The sob that Noah kept in fell loudly from his mouth. "She cannot be. She is not!"

"I am sorry…there is no way we can save her."

Noah's heart pounded hard against his chest as another sob escaped his mouth. Gently he pushed a lock of her red hair out of her face and behind her ear and held her close to his chest.

"I am sorry, my love. I have failed you."

Chapter Sixteen

Coldness. Darkness. Loneliness.

It was all Mary could sense. For a second Mary was paralyzed. She tried to move but could not do so. Everywhere hurt....

And finally her hand twitched and her body jerked upwards. Her eyes widened and she gasped trying to catch her breath. Pressing her palms to the ground she dug her fingers into the wet muddy, grassy ground. Quickly Mary stood up and peered around her surroundings. The fog drifted through the oak trees around. Looking down at herself she saw leaves and dirt stuck to the dress that she had thought was thrown away long ago. Taking a step forward a wave of dizziness overtook her. An intense pain shot through her head.

"Ow."

Mary pressed a hand to her forehead feeling a large welt on her head. She began making her way through the familiar woods.

Stepping out into the open the sun glared down at her. She winced, blocking her eyes from the sun. Her blossoming headache only grew worse as she peered around to see her neighborhood.

"I'm home."

A smile formed on her lips. But soon it faltered. Everything came back at once. Lotogettar. Tay kingdom. The dragon. Alexander...Noah. He was gone forever. She would never see him again. But what if it were not real? What if it was really a dream?

She ran past the park and down her street as tears blew off from her face. Minutes later she arrived at her house. It was the same as when she left it. The pink Cadillac was still there. And her bike that lay still in the grass.

Mary walked forward, stepping through the damp grass leading up to her front door.

What would her mom say when she answers? Would she be mad that she was gone for so long? Mary held her fist up ready to knock. Before she could, though, the door swung open.

"Mary!?"

Her mother gasped with tears in her eyes. Debbie appeared next to her and immediately pulled Mary into a hug.

"Oh my goodness! We have been so worried."

Mary stayed silent and turned to her mother who pulled her into a tight hug.

"Yesterday you left and never came back. We were about to go down to the police station and report you missing—you're a mess! I want you straight into the bath. We will talk after. Okay."

"I'm sorry."

"Don't apologize."

Rose teared up more and pulled Mary into the house. It felt weird to walk back into her house let alone her own room that she slept in for seventeen years.

Entering the bathroom Mary stared at her reflection in the mirror. She changed. Same face, different person. She fell in love and now her heart was broken because she will never see Noah again. Taking a deep breath a sudden sting shot through her stomach.

"Ow ow ow!" she gasped, bending over clutching her stomach.

"Honey, are you okay in there!?" Rose's voice sounded worried from the other side of the door.

"I-I'm fine," Mary called back and stood back up. She gripped the hem of her shirt pulling it up.

Right in the center of her stomach was a red scar the size of her finger. She grazed her finger over it, immediately regretting it as she hissed in pain rearing her hand back.

"It was real…."

***

"So you're really leaving."

"Yeah."

Two days had passed since Mary had arrived home.

Currently she stood outside with Max as Rose and Debbie packed the car with all her belongings. Somehow Rose convinced Mary to go to Florida and somehow Mary fell into the agreement. The pain in Mary's stomach was still there. She did her best at hiding the pain each step she took.

"I wish I didn't have to leave," Mary said, pulling Max into a tight embrace. He planted his head on top of hers.

"I'm going to miss you."

"Don't worry, Maxy. I'll come visit."

Max leaned down and kissed her forehead. "Goodbye…I love you."

Mary walked off to the car not hearing him whisper the last part.

"Bye, Mom. I'm sorry for what I said."

"Don't worry about that, my dear. I'm going to miss you."

Beep! Beep!

The car horn sounded.

"Go…you don't want to keep her waiting."

Mary nodded, waving goodbye as she hopped into the passenger seat next to her aunt. Debbie sighed at seeing her sad face as she began to drive down the street.

"Hey…don't worry. You'll get to see your boyfriend again when we visit in a couple months," Mary laughed

"He's not my boyfriend."

Her sad expression returned. Debbie felt a bit guilty for taking her away from her home.

"I loved someone else, but I'll never see him again."

They drove in silence for a while until Debbie pulled into a gas station.

"You wanna drive this thing?"

***

Mary had spent almost four hours driving through the night. Debbie was asleep and the faint noise of rock and roll music played from the radio. It had been a while since Mary heard real music. That was one thing she missed during her time in Lotogettar. But it could not lift her spirit. She was still depressed.

Noah could not get off her mind.

All her emotions that were bottled up finally hit her like a huge wave. The tears blurred her vision as they rolled quickly down her cheeks. A low sob fell past her lips. It felt like a chunk of her heart was cut out and burned to ashes.

She wanted to be back in his arms. She wanted him to kiss her and tell her everything is okay. But it wasn't okay. He wasn't there. He was in his home and she was back where she belonged. It could have never worked out.

Mary would never get over this. How could she?

A bright light shined in her eyes from a truck driving on the opposite side interrupting her thoughts. The truck grew closer within each second as tears continued to blur Mary's vision.

At that moment she did not know what she was doing when she removed her hands from the leather steering wheel. She closed her eyes as she lost all control of the vehicle.

Honk!!!!

The truck driver sent her a warning. But it was too late.

Crash!

Everything went dark. All her sadness and pain went away....

But it was not over just yet. Jolting up she gasped for air, clawing at her throat.

"My goodness…it's a miracle. You're awake!?"

To be continued....